T0090747

Rumi & Self Psychology

(Psychology of Tranquility)

Two astonishing perspectives for the discipline and science of self transformation: Rumi's Poetic language vs. Carl Jung's psychological Language.

Roya Rohani Rad, MA, PsyD

3rd Edition (Revised)

Disclaimer
The publisher and the author make an effort to give valid information to the public; however, they
make no guarantee with respect to the accuracy or completeness of the contents of the books published.
Science is unlimited, and there are many facts yet to be discovered and improved upon, as the world
expands. The information that SKBF Publishing presents to the public can only be used as a personal
enhancing device for building a healthy lifestyle. The reader is always responsible for using the
information the best possible way, according to his or her unique needs, environment, and personality.
Books, lectures, websites and other forms of self-help tools are general and valuable tools for a person
looking for self-education, but sometimes they are more like statistical information. They will give us
a general idea about most people, but we have to remember that each of us is a unique individual, and
treatment for our healing process would have to be administered accordingly.

Printed in Victoria, BC, Canada.

ISBN: 978-1-4269-2616-7 (sc)

*Our mission is to efficiently provide the world's finest, most comprehensive book publishing
service, enabling every author to experience success. To find out how to publish your book, your
way, and have it available worldwide, visit us online at www.trafford.com*

Trafford rev. 1/21/2010

Edited by: Walter L. Kleine, Kleine Editorial Services

SKBF Publishing (www.SKBFPublishing.com)

 www.trafford.com

North America & international
toll-free: 1 888 232 4444 (USA & Canada)
phone: 250 383 6864 ♦ fax: 812 355 4082

Contents

Dedication

I dedicate this book to all those deep thinkers who are true seekers of spirituality. I also dedicate it to all those who have inspired me one way or the other through their genuine acts or words.

<u>Note to the reader:</u> This book uses words us, our, we, they, or she as referring sources of explanation depending on what each section is trying to communicate with the reader. In addition, to lessen confusion, both he and she are being referred to as she. This is not a matter of preference but a matter of simplicity

Introduction

It seems that, in general, we as humans are more aware of physical pain than mental, emotional, or focal pain. If we have any kind of physical pain, we rush to a physician or a professional for help, or take the necessary steps to get better, but we tend to ignore our emotional pain, sometimes not even being aware of its existence. We assume, wrongly, that if we pay no attention to it, it will go away. However, just because we do not see something or are unaware of it does not mean that it is nonexistent. It is time for us to learn to dig in deeper into what cannot be seen by the five senses. It is time for us to act more as a multisensory human being, looking beyond the shallow.

Emotional and focal pains can express themselves in many forms, from depression, guilt, anxiety, fear, and anger, to resentment, hate, stress, low self-esteem, low motivation, and many other negative traits. All of these negative traits tend to block us from reaching our full potential, our center point, our balanced core, and finding our place in this life. In addition, they tend to block us from finding and feeling our being's harmony, and going through the process of achieving self-tranquility. They prevent us from achieving a sense of inner calmness, a state of being and living with no agitation or anxiety. That sense of inner freedom which is called tranquility.

Living with a sense of self-tranquility is a self-liberation. On the other hand, the opposite of self-tranquility is a blocked sense of self. A blocked sense of self is detrimental to the person, and to her surroundings. It has to be dealt with to find a cure for. In order to deal with emotional pain, one must first and foremost acknowledge that such pain really exists. To find ways for getting out of the denial of "not me," or "I don't have a problem," or, "it's others, not me." The next step is to admit that this emotional pain is real, to get ready for taking steps in curing it, and to develop a reasonable form of optimism so that one can grow beyond this pain. After that, the next steps are having determination and gaining knowledge, which are two essential factors for helping a person walk through the hallway of change and cure. Finally, one moves on to applying the knowledge in one's everyday life.

It is, after all, a continuous process. A person with an emotionally healthy pattern of behavior is able to feel her emotions, understands her true needs, values herself, is assertive, knows how to comfort herself, knows her boundaries in various relationships, and is respectful of herself and of others. In addition, a person with an emotionally healthy pattern of behavior is committed to her passions, practices self-discipline in various situations and attempts to be in control of her thoughts and behaviors, and allows herself to take risks while making mistakes, but, at the same time, is honest with herself for not repeating the same mistake twice.

At the beginning, walking through the process of tranquility and self-innovation imposes a number of different intense feelings on the person practicing it. For example, it may lead, at times, to a sensation of loneliness that one can be engulfed with; not necessarily a social kind of loneliness, meaning a lack of people, but a sense of inner loneliness. There may also be an intense sensation of anxiety, due to change. Every change brings about anxiety, because of the unknown. When we are experiencing a change, we are walking out of our comfort zone into a place that is challenging for us. As a result, we may experience some form of fear and discomfort. But, as we move forward, we get more comfortable with the new situation while finding new strength and skills through the experience.

In addition, during this change process, there may be some confusion because we are starting to think more deeply. There may be this intense thirst for knowing who we are. As teenagers, we start the process of forming our identity, and we start to think of what life means, who we are, what our role in life is, and many similar deep-rooted questions. During the course of our lifetime, if we mature emotionally, we are continuously seeking the one pathway that belongs only to us. This pathway is not imitated nor imposed; neither is it a fantasy based on irrational beliefs. It is a pathway that we have truly come to love and comprehend, because it belongs to us through reason, practice, and wisdom. We do not know where it may end. It seems continuous, but we feel like we belong there. Therefore, even during the sense of loneliness, there is a taste of joy, simply because there is awareness, hope, and acceptance. However, this is a true hope stemming from knowledge, not a false sense of delusional hope that we sometimes engage in to escape the challenges of reality.

There are many situations in which we may engage in a delusional hope. For example, a woman in an abusive relationship, who doesn't do anything about it and takes the abuse, destroys her inner self. All along, she says to herself, "It will get better," "This is so normal," "I deserve this," and "Everyone experiences that." Such a person does not stop once to ask how, why, and when changes are going to be implemented. Therefore, awareness of the situations we are in, walking out of the denial, not making excuses, and not giving delusional hope are all part of the process. Knowledge of truth in its deepest form is the goal of this process.

This book will use a combination of psychological and spiritual approaches in an attempt to face, and communicate with the reader, the reality of the deeper layers of a person's being; the self's different aspects. Hopefully, it will help the reader in understanding the concept of self. The meanings of the poems of Rumi, a 13th century Persian poet who is said to be one of the most popular poets in the West as well as the East, are explained in this book.

In addition, Carl Jung's concepts of self are combined in an attempt to form an explanation of an expanded and well-developed self. Jung was the Swiss psychiatrist who founded the concept of analytical psychology.

We will start the book with this poem from Rumi, which has been translated by Coleman Bark. In this poem, Rumi seems to be communicating the feelings of a person before and after she has discovered herself. He seems to be referring to the word "love" as a state of inner connection which brings peace in the form of feeling empty; empty of emotional imbalance, devoid of emotional turmoil and pain. It seems like Rumi's definition of love is a healthy sense of balanced connection with the inner self, the world, nature, and others; a connection away from any form of unhealthy, unsecured, and anxious attachments; a connection that is more of a detached compassion for any type of being; a connection away from neediness and the sole intention of personal satisfaction. A connection that is like a flow of energy between the subject and the object.

In this poem Rumi says:

Whoever finds love beneath hurt and grief
disappears into emptiness
with a thousand new disguises.
What is the soul?
What is the soul I cannot stop asking
if I could taste one sip of an answer
I could break out of this prison for drunks.
I didn't come here of my own accord
and I can't leave that way.
Whoever brought me here
will have to take me home.

The first chapter of this book will focus on Rumi's poems, and will attempt to compare some of his concepts with Jung's concept of self in psychology. The following chapters will discuss different self-expansion systems and psychological theories, including those of Jung. In each chapter inspiring quotes from popular figures, and poems by Rumi are related to the subject of that chapter. As Rumi says in the following poem, this book invites everyone who wants to truly find herself to start the process today.

Come, come, whoever you are.
Wonderer, worshipper, lover of leaving.
It doesn't matter.
Ours is not a caravan of despair.

Come, even if you have broken your vow a thousand times
Come, yet again, come, come

Chapter 1

Rumi & Concept of Self

Rumi was a 13th century poet whose poems have captivated many from all around the world. Rumi's poems seem to be a combination of what a scientist, scholar, lover, self-seeker, Sufi, Hindu, Jew, and Christian, among many others, are trying to communicate and are searching for. This can be seen in his writing:

Christian, Jew, Muslim, shaman, Zoroastrian, stone, ground, mountain, river, each has a secret way of being with the mystery, unique and not to be judged.

Rumi, because of his life's circumstances, traveled a great deal, having the opportunity to become familiar with various cultures and religions. He was a scholar, and familiarized himself with different aspects of science of his time. These could have been factors that contributed to Rumi's ability to identify with different groups and cultures which helped with the process of understanding differences and an expansion of mind, resulting in observation and learning rather than judgment. As a result, he might have been able to become more tolerant of people who were different from him. He seems to have been able to find more similarities than difference among people of different groups. He seems to value humans not according to any specific culture, religion, or anything in that nature, but rather according to how they valued their source of being and creation and how they connected with their true self. He seems to value awareness and have contempt for ignorance. These may have been the main reasons why Rumi felt such a deep connection to a man named Shams. Many of Rumi's poems show his love and connection to this man. A pure spiritual and emotional love that is deeply observed in Rumi's poems.

In his writings, Rumi's words seem to connect to the uppermost position of a human being. Rumi's world seems to be that of a fully developed human, that of the deepest layers of psychology that science has not yet reached, in some ways. It seems to be the world of a human who is mentally and spiritually advanced, and is not bound by social, personal, and cultural limitations. He seems to have a free and liberated mind, with no attachments, obsessions, irrationalities, etc. Therefore, it seems as if his poems and writings come from a pure source, a deep being, a mirror free of dust, a sky free of cloudiness, perhaps what Carl Jung would call the Collective Unconscious. That may be why so many people can identify with his poems and have their own personal interpretations of them depending on what stage of development they are at and what their needs are.

Today, Rumi's poems can be heard in many places throughout the world. It seems like one of the reasons for Rumi's reputation is that he is able to articulate the extremely personal and often mystifying world of the deepest layers of personal growth, the part that seems to be the core of everyone's being, and the different layers of the self. In his poems, Rumi seems able to communicate with everyone and to be able to touch the reader's innermost thoughts.

Relating Rumi's poems to the concept of the self, Rumi seems to have used a number of words that can be related to this concept. Words like self-worshipper, self-seeing, and self-knowing are used in his writings and poems. (1) Rumi views both the words self-worshipper and self-seeing in a negative light. He seems to relate a self-worshipper to someone who is conquered by the ego, or the less mature form of self. He seems to see a self-seeing person as someone who has an inflated and imaginary sense of self-importance, which turns into an elusive feeling of being better than others.

Rumi seems to use the word self-knowing in a constructive way, explaining that whoever knows herself is able to accept herself and knows her place in this world. It is not until one learns about who she is, what her weaknesses and strengths are, what her limitations are, and what her needs and character traits are that one is truly able to learn what her role is and what steps she is supposed to be taking.

Knowing our self involves seeing our self objectively. If we want to learn about who we really are we have to be honest with ourselves and not to use any justification or rationalizations to explain away our thoughts and behaviors as automatically right. We have to learn to recognize our own motivations and intentions for what they really are not what we present them to be.

Whatever level of self-knowledge we are in, we must look at ourselves as integral and multifaceted individuals. When we apply this awareness to our daily life, we come to realize and discover an authentic internal universe within us that can guide us to a more mature level of our self. In the more developed form of psychology, knowledge of oneself and self transformation is an unavoidable component.

Self reflection upon what one thinks, feels, and does creates a sense of awareness and self knowledge that is empowering. An internal sense of power that lessens insecurities and feelings of inadequacies. We need to become educated about a psychology towards the rejuvenation of our internal condition in order to renovate our traumas, complexes, hatred, phobias, anxieties, resentment and all sort of psychological flaws that cause us damages. Self psychology encourages us to go deep to the root of the problem within ourselves and to try to make an effort for the healing.

In psychology, the word self-worshipper, or self-narcissism, portrays the character trait of someone who has an exaggerated sense of self-love.

Freud, called the father of psychology, thought that a moderate degree of narcissism is necessary for all humans. He was the first to use this term in psychology. Many psychologists believe that a reasonable amount of healthy narcissism helps the individual fulfill her needs, but it has to be balanced. In psychology, excessive narcissism is diagnosed as a personality dysfunction and a disorder (Narcissistic Personality Disorder, or NPD).

This disorder is characterized as someone who has a grandiose sense of self-importance, and is preoccupied with fantasies of unlimited success, power, beauty, or ideal love. Other characteristics of NPD include excessive need for admiration, and taking undue advantage of others to meet one's needs through arrogance and excessive pride. These extreme forms of self-admiration may be the result of inner feelings of insecurity that could be rooted in childhood.

A moderate form of self-love and self-value is essential in the process of self-discovery. Someone who truly learns to know herself is more able to value her core being. This is where the concept of self-esteem arises. In psychology, self-esteem or self-worth is described as an individual's subjective evaluation of herself. It includes beliefs and emotions that are related to the individual. A person with a healthy sense of self-esteem starts to learn about herself and sees and accepts herself as an entity with strengths, weaknesses, potentials, and limitations. Self-esteem is a basic human need, and plays a paramount role in the progression of life. It is a nurturing force that helps the individual move forward rather than backward. One would be able to acknowledge her true value when she learns to acknowledge and discover her being's real meaning in this world. She is living in reality, rather than in fantasies. She is content to be who she is while being aware of her limits.

When it come to the concept of self, Rumi, continuously in his writings, seems to communicate a sense of self and the experience of love through this self. As an example of how Rumi seems to be expressing the concept of one's true being is this poem, translated by Nader Khalili. In this poem, Rumi seems to be encouraging the reader to become one, and to unite with her deeper sense of self instead of focusing on the basic level. A basic self, which is the one with unlimited desires, insecure attachments, projections, and insecurities can lead to destruction rather than production. It is only through connection with the deeper self that the door to truth will open to the person, and the person will be able to see the reality of life rather than living in illusion. In psychology, people are encouraged to function from their mature self while controlling the other aspects of this self (less mature forms). Rumi writes:

One went to the door of the Beloved and knocked.
A voice asked, 'Who is there?'
He answered, 'It is I.'
The voice said, 'There is no room for Me and Thee.'
The door was shut.
After a year of solitude and deprivation, he returned and knocked.
A voice from within asked, 'Who is there?'
The man said, 'It is Thee.'
The door was opened for him.

In another poem, translation by Shahram Shiva, Rumi writes:

When your chest is free of your limiting ego,
Then you will see the ageless Beloved.
You can not see yourself without a mirror;
Look at the Beloved, He is the brightest mirror.

Rumi in this poem seems to be pointing to a "limiting ego" and an "ageless lover." To related these poems to that of Carl Jung. Carl Jung explains that there are three levels of consciousness: Ego, Personal Unconscious, and Collective Unconscious. The Ego is the conscious level which carries out daily activities. This is everything that we are conscious of. All thinking, feeling, perceiving that we are aware of. Ego is not bad or good by itself. What makes it bad or good is whether we are in control of it or whether it is in control of us. If we focus too much on the ego, we are limiting ourselves and ignoring the rest of us. In addition, we may create an inflated ego.

The second level of consciousness, according to Carl Jung is the Personal Unconscious which is the individual's thoughts, memories, wishes, impulses. This is the information we have developed in conscious but has been repressed due to it being disturbing to us. It has been developed through personal experience. It is idiosyncratic

The third level of consciousness is the Collective Unconscious which is the storehouse of memories. These memories have been inherited from ancestors of the whole human race. This contains archetypes, emotionally charges images and thoughts form that have universal meanings. In addition, this is a collective experience that humans have had in their evolutionary past which is a result of common experiences. It is worth saying that even though, usually, humans are not consciously aware of this but it has a big part in their life.

When it come to the meaning of self, people have trying to comprehend and explain the experience of self for centuries. Many mystics and poets, as well as scientists and psychologists, have described the self in terms of the core of humanness. Rumi seems to be describing the experience of the self's various elements, and how acknowledging and finding this self, and all its elements and pieces, can help the person feel a sense of harmony, contentment, awareness, and wholeness. As we said earlier, from Rumi's poems, it seems like he is explaining the feeling one experiences when she connects to the deep levels of the self, nature, and creation. In psychology, people are encouraged to get to the roots of the suppressed memories of the unconscious. This unconscious is explained as one of the deepest layers of the person's psych.

We can categorize the self into different levels in order to be able to comprehend it better. These categories of the self have been named differently by different people, but, in general, there are three major ones.

The first level is the child-like self that corresponds to our body and the feelings attached to it. This has been called the natural self, the lower self, the basic self, or the child self, etc. We will call it the child self for the purpose of this book.

This level is below our conscious awareness, and is the one that gives us signals that arouse desires like sexual needs and basic pleasures of life. This level is also related to our feelings of pain, hunger, thirst, or any other forms of similar signals. This level of the self learns to do physical things, and by doing the same things over and over again, transforms them into habits. This child self works based on instant gratification, without the ability to delay an urge.

The next level of the self, the conscious self, is in charge of choosing and decision-making when the child self is responding to its desires and basic needs. If we ignore or do not acknowledge this conscious self, we will end up behaving in ways that may not be reasonable and may be damaging to us. This is because without the conscious self's interference, our child side is in action without supervision, continuously trying to fulfill desires without any consideration of short or long term consequences.

Loving ourselves and living a balanced lifestyle starts with paying attention to our child self with kindness and trying to discipline it at the same time. Then we can consciously teach, discipline, train, and format this child self to be a tool of support rather than a tool of blockage in our life. This child self, if trained and controlled, can work in harmony with the conscious self. This is where the processes of self-control and self-discipline come into play, which we will discuss in an upcoming chapter. It involves learning how to master this child self to open the door to finding harmony between different levels of our awareness and to be able to reach our full potential in life by balancing our energy and focus on what really matters, rather than wasting them on chasing every desire and urge that comes along the way.

As mentioned earlier, in psychology, different psychologists identified the various levels of the self differently. For example, Freud seem to have identified the child self as something similar to his definition of the Id, the conscious self as something similar to his definition of the Ego, and the higher self as something similar to his definition of the Super Ego.

Yet, there are other psychologists who have called this child self the child, the conscious self an adult, and the higher self a wise parent or guardian angel. In the end, it is not important how one names these parts. What's important is how one understands and responds to these parts. We all have a different way of learning, what matters is to be able to comprehend the message that is deep within each categorization. They all seem to have similar messages, some deeper, some not as deep.

During the course of life, we may get trapped in focusing too much on the basic levels of the self, the ego, and the basic needs. We may go through a lifetime denying the existence of any deeper being in us. Acknowledging all the denied parts and finding a way to harmonize these fragments are useful ways to allow them to express themselves in a person's life. If done properly and with determination, this sense of harmony brings a feeling of content which flows like a river in the Spring, meaning moderately and easily. This sense of being content comes from a sense of well-being that only the person experiencing it can describe. This feeling of being content comes with joy. However, it is important to note that this feeling does not leave out other feelings, like sadness, anger, or fear, but the joy increases when we are able to hold close these parts of ourselves and allow them to find their natural balanced position in our life. This brings about living in a state of awareness, being aware of all our parts, actions, intentions, thoughts, and behaviors as they happen, unfolding the mystery within. This is an experience, a process, not a thing. This is done only through self-application.

Another point worth mentioning is that we as humans seem to categorize everything as bad vs. good. The more limited we make ourselves to the world, the more specific this categorization becomes. We need to learn that there is no black and while thinking when it comes to bad or good, there is only in-balance or out-of-balance. The balance point is a center point that is unique to each individual. My balance point and center may not be the same as someone else. We all need to find our own balance point. To refer back to the previous statement about bad or good, for example, negative emotions like sadness, fear, and anger are normal situational responses. They are not bad emotions. A moderate level of these emotions is essential to survival. For example, it's normal to feel sad where we lose something of value. However, if the sadness takes too long and becomes too intense, it becomes a disorder called depression, which can haunt and prevent us from moving forward. That sadness then may become "bad" for that individual because it is out of balance. Yet another example, the emotion happiness is a normal emotion. But too much of it may create a manic human being.

Rumi refers to the word Spring in his writings. This word seems to be indicative of the state of mind and how we feel a sense of renewal as we let the experience of love flow through us, as we feel our emotions and let them be, and as we learn about ourselves and become more true to our state of being.

Some of Rumi's terms seem to be similar to Jung's concepts of the process of self-realization, which, according to him, is the goal of analytical psychology. Jung explains that during the process of self-realization, all the active fragments (archetypes) of the person's unconscious become combined with the self. The self should balance the power of these parts in order to achieve both unity and order. This is similar to Freud's concept that Ego must be powerful enough to deal with Super-Ego and Id, which are, according to Freud, different levels of human's psych.

An example of Rumi's concepts of self-realization can be seen in the following poem, translated by Shahram Shiva, in which Rumi seems to be communicating that finding one's true self and connecting with it will help the person find her role in life and her destiny.

When you find yourself with the Beloved,
embracing for one breath,
In that moment you will find your true destiny.
Alas, don't spoil this precious moment
Moments like this are very, very rare.

Referring back to Rumi's poems, and their meaning related to self psychology, Rumi's words seem to form a bridge between the east and the west. There are different interpretations of Rumi's poems that may be related to one's level of understanding of what he is trying to communicate, and one's personal belief and level of emotional and focal maturation.

One of the main differences between how people understand Rumi's poems seems to be reflected in the concept of love. Some western readers have been attracted by Rumi's use of romantic metaphors, which have caused him to be regarded as a poet of love. Rumi's mixed grasp of cultures and religions outside his own, and his knowledge of law, history, literature, and nature are contributing elements that have made his poems so captivating to the reader. The work of Rumi appears to have a purpose of communication with the Absolute, something superior, perhaps what Freud calls the super-conscious, what religious leaders call God, and what scientists are trying to discover. In his work, Rumi communicates what seems to be an attempt to put into language the nature and significance of the invisible universe, something that seems mysterious, yet very much a part of us, something that gives us great hope for moving ahead. For example, In *The Story of Solomon and the Hoopoe*, Rumi writes:

Do thou hear the name of everything from the knower? Hear the inmost meaning of the mystery of He That Taught the Names. With us, the name of everything is its outward appearance, with the Creator, the name of everything, as its inward reality.

Rumi's ability to bring to mind the ecstasy of nature and everyday life seems to be another captivating factor in his poems. He seems to be communicating with the reader that if one learns to focus on the present moment and to be aware of her emotions and her surroundings, every detail of life will be a satisfying and acceptable experience. This seems to be similar to psychotherapy techniques in which the concepts of relaxation, concentration, and challenging irrational pattern of thinking have been emphasized. In many forms of psychotherapy, the person is encouraged to focus on the here and now, and to learn ways to focus and concentrate. Individuals are encouraged to have a specific time and place where they think about how to solve problems in a productive way. Therefore, rather than spending a large portion of the time focusing on the problem itself, the time is spent on the solution. It's all about using our energy in the most productive way possible, and not wasting it.

Some of Rumi's poems communicate feelings of joy in being able to play a role in the natural process of life. In today's technologically and highly developed world, which seems to be socially fragmented at the same time, these forms of expressions are too rare.

As an example would be this poem in Mathnawi. (2)

My soul wants to fly away when your presence calls it so sweetly.
My soul wants to take flight, when you whisper, "Arise."
A fish wants to dive from dry land into the ocean, when it hears
the drum beating, "Return." A Sufi, shimmering with light, wants to
dance like a sunbeam when darkness summons him.

Rumi appears to communicate with the individual who has an increasing thirst for an instinctive, meaningful, and multifaceted response to everyday life; to have a more peaceful and purposeful daily existence functioning beyond the five senses. Rumi's love poems captivate readers for what seems to be today's lack of deep understanding of what it means to give love and to receive it, thereby referring to a sense of deep and productive connection. In today's world, concepts like insecure attachments, obsessions, temporary physical attractions, and a mind-numbing chain of weak moments are confused with love. Rumi appears to be communicating a true meaning of love that comes from a true sense of self-knowledge and feeling of security in this world and our place in it; one that is a genuine and a healthy connection to our surroundings, which brings about a true sense of physical, psychological, and focal balance and peace; one with less emotional ups and downs, and with more purpose and determination.

Another significance of Rumi's writings can be associated with today's distressing conditions of life. Similar to many people in the eastern and western worlds today, Rumi lived through astonishing social and political turmoil. His life was not far from ambiguity and danger, because of what seemed to be political instability, and also profound inner changes toward self-actualization. Many of these distressing life conditions and situations are expressed though his writings. He communicates, in many of his poems, how this pain caused by one's surroundings can engulf one's being. It seems that writing was a healing process for Rumi.

This chapter attempted to explain Rumi's writing related to self. In the following chapters, there will be more emphasis on the psychological aspects of self.

Chapter 2

Rumi and Carl Jung's Concept of Psych

This section will make an effort to integrate Rumi's concepts with those of Carl Jung, for a better understanding of the model of the psych in an individual. According to Jung, the purpose of life is to realize the self. This self is the sum of all opposites in individuals.

A person needs to learn all aspects of her personality, equally, to be able to learn about the self. For example, a person needs to be aware of her different elements, like male/female, ego/shadow, good/bad, conscious/unconscious, individual/whole, etc., to be able to experience her whole sense of self. One needs to acknowledge the opposites, and process any imbalance or denied parts in order to be able to accept them, have control over them, make them work in harmony, and move forward in life. Otherwise, the denied parts of the self will turn into suppressed memories that will drag the person into stages of deep denial and projection, which may result in pulling the person farther and farther away from experiencing her whole self. (3)

Referring to Rumi's writings, it seems like he also encourages the reader to experience her different parts and emotions. This poem seems to be telling the reader to bring out the child and the shadow side of the self similar to the concepts of Carl Jung and to accept them with love for a cure to happen. (4)

Cry Out in Your Weakness
Where lowland is,
that's where water goes. All medicine wants
is pain to cure . . . Tear the binding from around the foot
of your soul, and let it race around the track
in front of the crowd . . .
Give your weakness
to one who helps.
Crying out loud and weeping are great resources.
A nursing mother, all she does
is wait to hear her child.
Just a little beginning-whimper,
and she's there.
God created the child, that is, your wanting,
so that it might cry out, so that milk might come.
Cry out! Don't be stolid and silent
with your pain. Lament! And let the milk
of loving flow into you.

In the previous section we stated that Jung described the self's psyche as having three segments: The ego, the personal unconscious, and the collective unconscious.

In addition, we stated that according to Jung, the ego is identified as the conscious mind, and is closely associated with the personal unconscious (anything that is not conscious currently, but could be). This includes memories that are remembered and the ones that have been suppressed for some reason. Jung's third concept, which makes his theory stand out from all others, is called the collective unconscious. It is defined as something of a psychic inheritance. It is the pool of our experience as a species, something like a knowledge we are all born with, but are unable to be directly conscious of. However, it influences all our experiences, thoughts, and behaviors, through our emotions. (3 & 5)

Rumi's writings indicate that some of his experiences may have come from this collective unconscious, and that he seems to have been fully aware of them. Reading Rumi's poems may give the reader a sense of encouragement to experience her collective unconscious, too. In the following poem, for example, Rumi's way of expression refers to a deeper meaning of being. (6)

Stay Close, my Heart
Stay close, my heart, to the one who knows your ways;
Come into the shade of the tree that always has fresh flowers.
Don't stroll idly through the bazaar of the perfume-markers:
Stay in the shop of the sugar-seller.
If you don't find true balance, anyone can deceive you;
Anyone can trick out of a thing of straw,
And make you take it for gold
Don't squat with a bowl before every boiling pot;
In each pot on the fire you find very different things.
Not all sugarcanes have sugar, not all abysses a peak;
Not all eyes possess vision, not every sea is full of pearls.
O nightingale, with your voice of dark honey! Go on lamenting!
Only your drunken ecstasy can pierce the rock's hard heart!
Surrender yourself, and if you cannot be welcomed by the Friend,
Know that you are rebelling inwardly like a thread
That doesn't want to go through the needle's eye!
The awakened heart is a lamp; protect it by the hem of your robe!
Hurry and get out of this wind, for the weather is bad.
And when you've left this storm, you will come to a fountain;
You'll find a Friend there who will always nourish your soul.
And with your soul always green, you'll grow into a tall tree,
Flowering always with sweet light-fruit, whose growth is interior.

In another poem, which follows, Rumi seems to encourage the reader to feel the ups and downs of life, and those of the experience of self. He seems to be communicating that there have to be states of contracting and expanding in a balanced manner for what he calls "the fist opening up" to happen. This could mean that if one wants to move up the ladder of the self-knowledge and reach her full self, one should accept these contractions and expansions, because they go together. Sometimes, the contraction may be painful . But valuable things in life usually don't come easily. After each contraction comes an expansion. One cannot have one without the other. One has to learn to step out of the comfort zone, which is not an easy process. There is the fear of the unknown. There are the challenges of the adjustment phase, but if one knows what one is doing, one is willing to accept all these challenges because then one is sure there is light at the end of this tunnel. Moving forward with determination, awareness, and willingness to accept changes. In the following poem Rumi seems to be saying that self-growth is like a bird trying to learn how to fly. There are risks of falling, but the bird does not care. She only has one thing in mind, and that is to fly. After determination comes the joy of reaching the goal. The question for us is whether the goal we choose is worth the effort and how deep were we aiming? Are we continuously pointing toward satisfying impulses, unlimited desires, and the five senses or are we in search of something more profound.

Bird wings
Your grief for what you've lost lifts a mirror
up to where you're bravely working.
Expecting the worst, you look, you look, and instead,
here's the joyful face you've been wanting to see.
Your hand opens and closes and opens and closes.
If it were always a fist or always stretched open,
you would be paralyzed.
Your deepest presence is in every small contracting
and expanding, the two as beautifully balanced and coordinated as
bird wings. *

Let us refer back to Jung's concepts of the self, and to learn more about the self's limitless and extraordinary elements. Jung introduced the term "shadow," and identified it as anything that is unconscious, repressed, undeveloped, and denied by the individual. Everyone, according to Jung, has a shadow, and acknowledging and learning about it is essential to reaching a whole sense of self. To elaborate, let's use an example. Almost all of us are familiar with situations in which we felt uncomfortable or even irritated by the presence of another person.

Whenever an action, quality, or characteristics in another person bring about strong emotional reactions in us, we can be sure that we are feeling a part of our own shadow which we may be projecting into another. These qualities may be the exact opposite of what we think we may have, but, surprisingly, we have them. We're just not aware of them. On the other hand, a person who has a positive side of our shadow will draw us toward herself or may even make us fall in love with her/him. This could be what is called the good part of our shadow. This is our psyche's way of bringing itself into our awareness and consciousness. (3) We have to pay attention to these signals that our psych is continuously giving us, we have to learn to respond to them, or they will be wasted. They are there for a reason. They are communicating with us what we don't know about ourselves. Ignoring and avoiding these signals will only make the source denser.

As another example, we have all come across people we thought were acting too nice. Something tells us that this may not be their true self, or that they are acting fake, in some ways, when we are around them. These are the type of people who may be buried behind a mask of what Jung would call a persona; a false portrayal of the self. These types of people will intentionally avoid any kind of negative emotion, or even behavior. Denying these emotions will suppress them and make them thicker, while dragging the person into a state of deception to herself and others. As said before, we should learn, recognize, and process every aspect of our shadow including the dark side to be able to control it. As Jung says, "whatever one does not live, lives against one." If we learn about them, then we can learn how to be in control of them. If we deny their existent, then we are letting them be in control of us.

To refer back to human's different elements; it may be useful to refer to the term mechanism. Let's start with an example, sometimes we may feel like we are all continuously dragged by other people wanting to fulfill their desires and to get something from us that would benefit them. Our unconscious motive is to satisfy others, and that part may lead us to become a people pleaser, someone who will often have conflicts with her own basic needs. In addition to that, the physical world's accidents and natural disasters will make it necessary for us to learn ways to deal with emotional conflict. Freud's term for ways of dealing with emotional conflict is "mechanisms."

Modern psychology calls it a defense mechanism, in both pathological and everyday settings. (7) There are primary defenses and there are secondary ones which are more complex for a more matured human. There are many defense mechanisms that we, as humans, used as children for our mental and physical protection. But, as we mature, we need to learn ways to outgrow these mechanisms.

Projection and denial are two of these defense mechanisms. Denial is a common defense mechanism which is an automatic response to avoid something uncomfortable causing rejection of the truth. For example, a child who does something bad would deny doing it to avoid punishment or would explain the bad behavior in a positive way to escape any negative consequences. Denial is painful and causes frustration for people surrounding the person who denies she has a weakness she needs to work on. Denial is a defense mechanism of an immature mind.

Projection is another unconscious defense. We project onto others the parts of ourselves that we deny the existence of. There are many immature and undeveloped fragments of our self that we keep hidden, and are unaware of. The reason for this is that we are trying to keep our image together, and therefore we deny that we have these parts.

Our desire and intent is to be accepted by others; family, society, peers, and environment. We should, however, be aware of the fact that if these parts are hidden within the subconscious, it does not mean that they are not active in our life. They are very much active, but have control over us rather than us having control over them. Jung said that everyone carries a shadow, and the less it is embodied in the individual's conscious life, the blacker and denser it is, on all counts. It forms an unconscious snag, thwarting our most well-meant intentions.

We need to ask ourselves if it's time for us to work on each piece of our being and walk through the process of self-liberation. Until then, a sense of true self-knowledge, which will bring about a sense of inner balance and peace will seem far away. It is only through self-discovery that one feels connected to all her elements and her source and will have a sense of liberation. An inner liberation comes only after one learns to be in control of this self's elements and the thoughts, emotions, behaviors that accompany them. An inner liberation is not being boundless, careless, fruitless, and sluggish. It is being disciplined and in control of the self. In addition, it is being focused, determined, and full of passion; it is not being manipulated by outside forces, insecure and anxious attachments based on neediness, wasteful instant gratifications, and endless addictive desires.

Rumi's poems seem to express these same concepts of experiencing different parts and feelings, to be able to let go of the emotional agony that has been brought upon us by blockages, and to be able to free ourselves from the emotional roller coaster.

An example would be this poem:

How long can I lament with this depressed heart and soul
How long can I remain a sad autumn
Ever since my grief has shed my leaves
The entire space of my soul is burning in agony
How long can I hide the flames wanting to rise out of this fire
How long can one suffer the pain of hatred of another human
A friend behaving like an enemy with a broken heart
How much more can I take the message from body to soul
I believe in love
I swear by love
Believe me my love
How long like a prisoner of grief can I beg for mercy
You know I'm not a piece of rock or steel
But hearing my story even water will become as tense as a stone
If I can only recount the story of my life
Right out of my body flames will grow

When we are able to acknowledge, learn about, and accept all the different parts of ourselves, the process of connecting with our true self and our source, and learning about it, will flow more naturally. This sense of connection helps us form a healthy connection with our surroundings, something that Rumi constantly writes about.

In the following poem about love at the end of this chapter, Rumi seems to be communicating the feeling one gets when one is able to truly experience love, a healthy sense of connection rather than an insecure and anxious attachment. As mentioned, Rumi's concept of love seems to be more than that of a sexual, physical, and emotional attachment. It is a deep sense of inner connection, which results in a deep sense of outer connection. (7) An outer connection to others, nature, creator, and being; more of a detached connection.

To understand what Rumi may have been experiencing through this love that he expresses throughout his writings, we may want to look at what the word love and the experience of loving may mean. We will refer to Lee's 6 styles of love for the purpose of the content of this book. Lee reported that there are 6 styles of love. Eros, Ludus, Storge, Pragma, Mania, and Agape.

The first type of love is Eros. Eros love is a passionate love without obsessions, it is more sensual and based on chemistry. An Eros lover knows what physical features s/he is looking for in a partner and goes after them. This type of love is more of a romantic love, looking more for chemistry. In this type of love, the lovers are more likely to fall in love quickly. Eros lover focuses intensely on the love and does not push but allows the development of love. It is based on high self esteem and self confidence. There is a sense of passionate physical and emotional love based on aesthetic satisfaction categorized more into the romantic love. This type of love is based on an esthetic satisfaction. The advantage of Erotic love is its sentimentality and being relaxing, the disadvantage is the anticipated perishing of attraction and perhaps living in a fantasy or unrealistic world.

The second type of love is the Ludos love. Ludos is the game playing type of love based on having fun, an activity, quantity not quality. Ludic lovers change a large number of partners or may have more than one at a time but Ludic lovers do not wish to hurt anyone and are open and honest about their taste of love. They only want to enjoy life. The advantage of Ludic love is its enjoyable sexual and sensual practices, the disadvantage is the likelihood of unfaithfulness or getting board with a partner too quickly while s/he is not ready therefore hurting her/him.

The third type of love is Manic. Manic lovers have many passionate love (Eros) qualities but are more unstable and hesitant. Manic lovers crave for love but are jealous and doubtful. They tend to force and push their partners into commitments which may lead to relationship problems and grieving for the manic lover. This type of love is fueled by low self esteem and neediness. This type of love is a highly volatile love with obsession which is fueled by low self-esteem. The advantage of Manic love is its intensity but the disadvantage of it is the jealousy, neediness, obsession and instability and the potential for being codependent and addicted to the partner.

The fourth type of love is the Storge. Storge love is a type of friendship love with strong affection but not much passion. This type of a relationship is strong, secure and both partners share similar values. Storge love focuses on long-term commitment and looks at passion, lust and sex as secondary (or maybe none). This type of love develops slowly and starts with friendship. The advantage is intimacy, the disadvantage is the lack of passion.

The fifth type of love is Pragma. Pragma love is a very practical type of love. A Pragmatic lover evaluates potential partners carefully with more focus on a good match on many aspects rather than just the passion and pleasure. There are conditions involved with a Pragmatic lover. This love is more driven by the head than the heart and the Pragmatic lover is thinking rationally of their expectations. They want to find similar values and reach a common goal with their partner. The advantage of Pragmatic love is its practicality and the fact that it is more realistic, the disadvantage is what may seem like a lack of emotion and demonstrations of affection.

Finally, the sixth type of love is Agape. Agape love is an altruistic and unconditional love. For an Agapic lover there is less emphasis on passion and sexuality and more emphasis on self sacrifice for the other. This is a rare type of love which is a spiritual motherly love, selfless, self sacrificing. The advantage of this love is generosity, the disadvantage may be feelings of guilt or incompetence in the partner if not synchronized. (8)

One might want to add a seventh type of love to Lee's styles which is a balanced combination of all of the six in the form of wholeness. The one important thing to consider when it comes to any type of love is that there has to be a sense of synchronization between the lovers; in other words, there has to be a concord between the lover and the object of love for any source of healthy connection to occur. To go back to Rumi's poem about love, this poem seems related, it says:

Through love all that is bitter will be sweet
Through Love all that is copper will be gold.
Through Love all dregs will turn to purest wine
Through Love all pain will turn to medicine.
Through Love the dead will all become alive.
Through Love the king will turn into a slave
Love is the Master
Love is the One who masters all things;
I am mastered totally by Love.
By my passion of love for Love
I have ground sweet as sugar.
O furious Wind, I am only a straw before you;
How could I know where I will be blown next?
Whoever claims to have made a pact with Destiny
Reveals himself a liar and a fool;
What is any of us but a straw in a storm?
How could anyone make a pact with a hurricane?
God is working everywhere his massive Resurrection;
How can we pretend to act on our own?
In the hand of Love I am like a cat in a sack;
Sometimes Love hoists me into the air,
Sometimes Love flings me into the air,
Love swings me round and round His head;
I have no peace, in this world or any other.
The lovers of God have fallen in a furious river;
They have surrendered themselves to Love's commands.
Like mill wheels they turn, day and night, day and night,
Constantly turning and turning, and crying out.
Take away everything that takes me from you.

Quotes

The true value of a human being is determined primarily by the measure and the sense in which he has attained liberation from the self.
Albert Einstein

Man unites himself with the world in the process of creation.
Erich Fromm

Man's main task in life is to give birth to himself.
Erich Fromm

As human beings, our greatness lies not so much in being able to remake the world—that is the myth of the atomic age—as in being able to remake ourselves.
Gandhi

The mainspring of creativity appears to be the same tendency which we discover so deeply as the curative force in psychotherapy, man's tendency to actualize himself, to become his potentialities. By this I mean the organic and human life, the urge to expand, extend, develop, mature,the tendency to express and activate all the capacities of the organism, or the self.
Carl Rogers

Happiness belongs to the self-sufficient.
Aristotle

Chapter 3

Toward Self Discovery

Rumi's writings and poems seem to be coming from a person who has been successful in the process of self discovery. His words can be used for any person who is going through the same process to feel his experience, and to get a sense of realistic hope. His words seem to be coming from a pure core with no need for irrationality and bias due to power struggles. Furthermore, it seems to be coming from a sense of inner connection with something magnificent, something that we all seem to have but mostly are ignorant and unaware. This sense of being uninformed about our core being could be due to the fact that we have not taken the necessary steps to walk thought the self-discovery process.

To discuss the process of self discovery, Jung explained humans in analytical terms, some of which are rated into the following categories. Jung stated that humans have higher-level needs, which he called spiritual needs, as much, if not more than, the basic biological needs. These higher needs pull individuals toward the search for the meaning of life. A thirst for knowing the deeper truth, an understanding of what lies beneath the surface. Using our five senses, we are able to see the surface; using the multi sensory system, however, we may become capable of looking into the deep. We may be able to look beyond behaviors into intentions behind them, to look beyond incidents into their cause, to look beyond surface into the roots.

Carl Jung also stated that there are categorizations to personality types and there are deeper meanings with identifications and categorizations of these personality types. Jung developed a personality typology which begins with the distinction between introversion and extroversion. According to Jung, introverts prefer their internal and core world of thoughts, feelings, fantasies, dreams, and so on. On the other hand, extroverts prefer the external world of things, other people, and activities.

These two words of introvert and extrovert have been confused with sociability, shyness, and things of that nature. This may be due to the fact that introverts tend to appear shyer and extroverts tend to appear more sociable. But Jung intended for these terms to refer more to whether one's ego is more often functioning from the persona and outer reality, or toward the collective unconscious and its archetypes. If we look at it from that perspective, the introvert could be more mature than the extrovert. It is worth mentioning that the Western culture seems to value the extrovert more, while the Eastern culture has the tendency to value introvert more heavily. However, Jung reported and warned that that we all tend to value our own type most, the type that we are mostly used to. Therefore, we have to be aware of the bias this may cause in our interactions with others.

Jung further said that people who are identified as introverts try to harmonize their inner conflicts into a whole self. Those who are identified as extroverts try to harmonize the self with social realities. When it comes to the process of self discovery, it may be useful for one to know whether she is more of an introvert or an extrovert. Then, the person can decide how this is effecting her process of wholeness and, if necessary, to try to balance these two to get closer to her center and whole self.

We discussed the conscious self, in the previous chapter. To elaborate and relate it to the content of this chapter, the conscious self is supposed to become the dominant self and take charge of the child self as the person grows. The seed of this stage is supposed o be planted at about age 7. This is done by the person learning, first through parents or caregivers and then by herself, on a continuous basis, making choices, and experiencing the consequences of each choice with awareness. Knowing oneself means discovering and acknowledging the parts which result in the conscious self becoming more aware of one's characteristics and eccentricities, and realizing that every person is a unique individual, with different challenges in life, and realizing that this conscious self has the potential to take charge of the decision-making process. These are important aspects of self discovery. The conscious self can direct the learning process by searching for and analyzing experiences and facts which will help in achieving one's goals in life.

As described in the previous chapter, Jung also discussed the term shadow, a part that humans are not aware of because they tend to deny it exists. It is like an area of a person's being that is a place for the repressed memories, feelings, and thoughts. The shadow is denied because it may contain the dark and painful points of our personality; parts that we have been encouraged to hide.

Shadow is the phenomenon whereby parts of one's personality, which are as real and concrete as arms and legs, remain outside one's experience. The problem with these renounced elements is that, while they are out of our consciousness, they still have a deep, and many times negative, influence on the way we behave, interact with others, and experience our lives. The negative influence is due to the fact that we are not aware of them.

One of the most important defense mechanisms we need to learn about and pay attention to when are acknowledging the shadow is projection. Projection is a defense mechanism in which we seem to refuse to accept the existence of certain elements within ourselves, therefore, forcing ourselves to project them onto other people. How often have we heard someone speaking in awed tones of someone else, when, from our point of view, they could be describing themselves?

Humans are composed of opposite forces of personality, which contain both unconscious and conscious possessions. If one disregards one of these forces, she cannot feel her true and whole self, because she is blocking herself and her full potential. The objective of mental/spiritual development is wholeness and balance, not perfection. The need for perfection may be coming from an inner hole that need attention. In reality, there is no perfection, since everything is constantly changing and evolving. There is, however, balance, which means to find harmony between each opposite side of ourselves, by learning about them, becoming aware of them, and acknowledging our being as a whole. Examples of a list of opposites, which was touched on in the previous chapter, can include conscious-unconscious, weakness-strengths, rational-irrational, extrovert-introvert, masculine-feminine, birth-death, animal-spiritual, think-feel, sense-intuit, etc. Balancing these different parts and finding a harmony between them should be the goal of a person seeking self-actualization and self-discovery. At the end, this process should help the person get closer to her center wherever that might be.

Therefore, the goal is consistency, not completion. This can also be seen in mathematics, in which Goedel's Proof states if arithmetic is consistent, then it is incomplete; but if complete, it is inconsistent.

Working with and acknowledging the shadow parts of ourselves enable us to understand and heal the wounds that caused the repression that is deep inside us. This process enables us to become more of who we really are, moving toward our authentic personality with an authentic inner power and inner control. A sense of inner control will lessens a need for an outer control. We do not want to repeat the unconscious patterns of behaviors that are unproductive. The more we move toward our genuine personality, the more we have access to a greater depth of meaning in our everyday lives.

The therapeutic and self-healing processes work to develop the central point of the unconscious, both up and down, accepting more of the unacceptable elements of ourselves into who we are. Meanwhile, we experience more richness in our lives, accompanied by more joy. It seems like we experience feelings more intensely and more broadly. But we don't try to escape these feeling, we are aware of their existence. The following poem seems to reflect what was discussed above. In this poem, Rumi seems to be communicating to the reader that the state of denial and ignorance and the lack of awareness brings about all these pains and suffering for us, and that waking up from that state will end this suffering and emotional pain. (9)

The Progress of Man
First he appeared in the realm inanimate;
Thence came into the world of plants and lived
The plant-life many a year, nor called to mind
What he had been; then took the onward way
To animal existence, and once more
Remembers naught of what life vegetive,
Save when he feels himself moved with desire
Towards it in the season of sweet flowers,
As babes that seek the breast and know not why.
Again the wise Creator whom thou knowest
Uplifted him from animality
To Man's estate; and so from realm to realm
Advancing, he became intelligent,
Cunning and keen of wit, as he is now.
No memory of his past abides with him,
And from his present soul he shall be changes.
Though he is fallen asleep, God will not leave him
In this forgetfulness. Awakened, he
Will laugh to think what troublous dreams he had.
And wonder how his happy state of being
He could forget, and not perceive that all
Those pains and sorrows were the effect of sleep
And guile and vain illusion. So this world
Seems lasting, though 'tis but the sleepers' dream;
Who, when the appointed Day shall dawn, escapes
From dark imaginings that haunted him,
And turns with laughter on his phantom griefs
When he beholds his everlasting home.

Quotes

Everything that irritates us about others can lead us to an understanding of ourselves.
Carl Jung

Remember, the entrance door to the sanctuary is inside you.
Rumi

What was said to the rose that made it open was said to me here in my chest.
Rumi

Your vision will become clear only when you look into your heart. Who looks outside, dreams. Who looks inside, awakens.
Carl Jung

Man's main task in life is to give birth to himself.
Erich Fromm

To know that you do not know is the best. To pretend to know when you do not know is a disease.
Lao Tzu

Chapter 4

Toward Self-Actualization

Rumi's words seem to be coming from a person who psychologists call a self-actualized person. Self-actualization is a process first described by a psychologist named Maslow. There have been some additions to the term since then, but, in general, it refers to people who welcome reality and facts rather than rejecting the truth, who have high peak experiences, and are relatively tolerant of themselves and others. It seems that humans have a natural tendency toward self-actualization, in order to develop their potential, so that they feel an enhanced sense of self. This natural tendency encourages a sense of equivalence within the person. An equivalence that gives the person a sense of inner peacefulness.

Self-actualization is considered to be a more mature way of comprehending life as it unfolds. Self-actualized individuals seem to have a sense of purpose for life, genuine interpersonal relationships that are meaningful in quality, not quantity, consequential activities, logical ways of thinking, ability to identify with higher human values, and self-respect. Individuals functioning at this level seem to have moved beyond the ego-oriented needs of Maslow's hierarchy to identify more with their sense of higher self. Maslow's hierarchy will be explained in chapter 11.

Further, self-actualized individuals tend to focus most of their time in the present. They have learned ways to cope with past memories that might have been negative, letting go of the resentments and anger, or any other negative emotions related to these memories. They seem to see life as a continuum, and seem to be more aware of how their life is unfolding and how it is evolving toward a profound purpose, resulting in a more logical acceptance of what is to come. They seem to be more in tuned with reality as it unfolds rather than living in a fantasy world with unrealistic expectations and constant struggle to satisfy basic needs.

Self-actualized people tend to have inner-directed, independent, and self-supportive behaviors. They seem to have less need for approval from other people because they have found ways to accept themselves. They accept all of themselves, strengths or weaknesses, and have found a way to understand that only with acceptance change is possible. They understand that no one can change though being in denial. They don't function from other people's expectations and perceptions but only those of themselves. This does not mean that they are not concerned, and neither does it mean that they are not connected with other peoples' matters, but it does mean that their decisions are made from their own core of consciousness. People who have been able to get to this level of maturation follow their own inner vision, have fewer needs and attachments, are not very concerned with results, have their own definition of what is productive for them, and are aware of the choices and the effect these choices have on them and the world. In addition, they are willing to take responsible risks.

The main blockages to self-actualization are fear of challenge, irrational beliefs, and lack of knowledge about self and surroundings, and the inability to apply the knowledge to make the self grow intellectually, emotionally, mentally, and spiritually. To deal with the fear of challenges, we should understand that, like all other emotions, fear in balanced form is useful for our survival and development. In the right capacity, fear is an emotion we need, but too much of it can prevent us from doing things that might be necessary or productive for our life. It could also prevent us from doing things that might seem uncertain or risky.

There are rational and irrational fears. For example, fear of snakes is a rational fear that keeps us safe from being hurt by them. However, we have to learn ways to let go of our irrational fear. This can be accomplished by learning the root of the fear, visualizing how our life will change if we challenge that irrational fear; challenging the irrationality with more rational ways of thinking, and finally with facing the fear. Reasonable fear is a necessity, unreasonable fear is an obstruction.

When it comes to self-actualization, behaviors that go against the individual's actualizing predisposition generate inadequacy in the sense of self. Individuals sometimes use defenses to escape the fear or discomfort they may face in their lifetime. They may twist perceptions of reality to reduce what they see as a threat, or they can act in ways that avoid becoming aware of the threatening experiences, for example, by ignoring or denying it. We can see people who blame their failures on causes outside themselves while crediting themselves for their successes. These behaviors may lead to self-handicapping strategies that prevent the individual from walking away from that which is unproductive, the comfort zone, and the zone that the individual gets used to but is unhealthy for her. This by itself creates the inability to move up the ladder of being toward maturity.

In the following poem, it seems like Rumi is looking more deeply into the reality of being, going from the physical senses to mental/emotional/focal levels of the self, to be able to experience a true feeling of joy. (9)

This is the experience of a self actualized human.

The drum of the realization of the promise is beating, we are sweeping the road to the sky.
Your joy is here today, what remains for tomorrow?
The armies of the day have chased the army of the night.
Heaven and earth are filled with purity and light.
Oh! Joy for he who has escaped from this world of perfumes and color!
For beyond these colors and these perfumes, these are other colors in the heart and the soul.

Oh! Joy for this soul and this heart who have escaped the earth of water and clay.

Although this water and this clay contain the hearth of the philosophical stone.

If thou wilt be observant and vigilant, thou wilt see at every moment the response to thy action.

Be observant if thou wouldst have a pure heart, for something is born to thee in consequence of every action.

Quotes

Man's ideal state is realized when he has fulfilled the purpose for which he is born. And what is it that reason demands of him? Something very easy—that he live in accordance with his own nature.
Seneca

Probably the authentic person is complete or final in some sense; he certainly experiences subjective finality, completion or perfection at times; and he perceives it in the world. It may turn out that only peakers can achieve full identity; that non-peakers must always remain incomplete, deficient, striving, lacking something, living among means rather than among ends; or if the correlation turns out not to be perfect, I am certain at least that it is positive, between authenticity and peak-experiencing.
Abraham Maslow

One of the greatest limitations in our world of philanthropy is the lack of understanding that there is, within each person, a yearning to be part of something larger than ourselves. Recognizing that need and meeting it is the reward of our ministry for humankind.
Arthur C. Frantzreb

The mainspring of creativity appears to be the same tendency which we discover so deeply as the curative force in psychotherapy, man's tendency to actualize himself, to become his potentialities. By this I mean the organic and human life, the urge to expand, extend, develop, mature, the tendency to express and activate all the capacities of the organism, or the self.
Carl Rogers

Chapter 5

Toward Self Liberation

Rumi's poems seem to be a manifestation of a person who is experiencing a liberated and free sense of self. A free and liberated self does not imply a person who has no boundaries and lacks self-discipline. On the other hand, self-discipline is essential for a contented life, and a contented life is fundamental to a person seeking self-liberation. To get to true freedom of the self, one needs to learn to control herself and to respect her boundaries, which will help her in respecting those of others. A boundary-less self is a perplexed being who does not know her role in life, one who feels overwhelmed and confused over what her life beholds, one who continuously feels like others are taking advantage of her, causing her to have intense negative emotions, and one who is constantly weighed down by life.

A truly free self is free of insecure, avoidant, and unbalanced attachments and harmful desires that control her sense of being. A free self is in control of her emotions, her thoughts, and her behaviors not the other way around. She is not a slave but a master of her existence. It is a self that has the freedom to make right decisions for her life to be able to be a productive person functioning with her full potential.

It is a self that is far away from taking advantage and abusing her surroundings; one who gives as much, if not more than, she receives from the world.

We referred to the word attachment. When it comes to self-liberation, a liberated self lets go of attachments and replaces them with healthy love and connection that flows naturally.

The word "attachment" could be classified in different aspects. There are secure and healthy attachments, in the form of productive connections that may lead to feeling good, feeling supported, feeling wanted, and feeling a sense of an unconditional love. These forms of healthy attachments are more of detached connections which are continuously generating love and productivity.

There are, however, negative and harmful types of attachments, like anxious and avoidant attachments, which can become obstacles that get in a person's way of getting to her true and fulfilled self. For example, an obsessed and controlling husband who has anxious attachments toward his wife and is scared of losing her, or a mother with a fragmented sense of self, who is constantly controlling her child and preventing her from full emotional, mental, and focal growth.

Some researchers believe that the first category of attachment, secure attachment, is not categorized as an attachment but as a healthy connection. This perspective views all forms of attachments in a negative light, because if it is healthy, then it is not an attachment. We are not supposed to be clinging to others only to satisfy our needs and compensate for our insecurities. We are supposed to connect with others to relate and create a mutual feeling of love and respect. This view indicates that as children, we need to be attached to a protective object because we do not have necessary physical/emotional/mental tools to take care of ourselves. But once we make mental and emotional progress in life and mature in all these aspects, we need to let go of these attachments and become more self-contained. Where that level of maturity is reached, there are no more needs for attachments.

To elaborate on the discussion of attachment and its concept, as reported earlier, in psychological terms there are different categories. We briefly discussed the separate categories, but will explain these in terms of an adult who has these attachments.

The first category, called secure adults, are those who have a sense of healthy connection, have an easier time getting closer to others, and feel more comfortable when others get close to them. They do not worry about being abandoned, and have an easier time letting go of a relationship that is not functional.

The second categories, avoidant adults, are somehow uncomfortable being close to others, trusting others, and getting intimate.

The third category, anxious and ambivalent adults, find that others are unwilling to get as close as they would like them to, often worry that the significant other doesn't really love them, and want to cling completely with the other person, which can scare the other person away.

So, the first category seems to be a much healthier form of attachment, which as said before is referred to mostly as a connection rather than an attachment. Rumi seems to communicate this in his poems. He seems to be encouraging the reader to find a healthy sense of connection rather than a damaging attachment.

A healthy sense of connection can generate a sense of freedom and love for the parties involved, in which no one feels controlled and where compromises are made out of love, not fear.

A free and liberated self connects; she does not attach nor clings. When it comes to connecting it may be relative to discuss the term love one more time but from another view. Love, according to many psychologists, consists of three components. These components are intimacy, commitment, and passion. A productive form of love is the one that forms a system in which everyone feels positive and benefits from each other, and the system becomes productive and positive for everyone. It is also one in which everyone gives and receives in a natural way. It will help form a system in which its members can gain emotional, physical, and spiritual nurturing for development.

In a relationship with a healthy sense of connection, members help each other by helping in the fulfillment of each other's needs instead of blocking each other's growth.

A free and liberated self has been able to master her basic needs. Need can be explained as a psychological trait that provokes an individual to move and to take steps for reaching a goal, which guides the person in having a sense of direction for her behavior. People have a wide variety of needs, ranging from basic to advanced, for example, from hunger to security to self-actualization.

Some needs are more powerful than others. The lower forms of needs are similar to those of animals, but only humans have higher needs. A person who is self-liberated is one who is free of insecure attachments and lower forms of excessive needs. A self-liberated individual would still have needs, but they are in a very balanced form and less of an animalistic and primitive nature. They have been able to outgrow the basic needs as they matured intellectually, emotionally, mentally, and spiritually.

In the following poem, Rumi seems to be encouraging the reader to free herself from imitation of irrational patterns of thinking and behavior, even if they have been imposed on her by people who did it out of love, but without knowledge (for example one's parents). In addition, one seems to be encouraged to get out of the comfort zone and move forward and face the fear that comes with it to be able to walk toward a sense of self liberation. (3)

This World Which Is Made of Our Love for Emptiness
Praise to the emptiness that blanks out existence. Existence:
This place made from our love for that emptiness!
Yet somehow comes emptiness, this existence goes.
Praise to that happening, over and over!
For years I pulled my own existence out of emptiness.
Then one swoop, one swing of the arm, that work is over.
Free of who I was, free of presence, free of dangerous fear, hope, free of mountainous wanting.
The here-and-now mountain is a tiny piece of a piece of straw blown off into emptiness.
These words I'm saying so much begin to lose meaning:
Existence, emptiness, mountain, straw:
Words and what they try to say swept out the window, down the slant of the roof.
I've said before that every craftsman searches for what's not there to practice his craft.
A builder looks for the rotten hole where the roof caved in. A water-carrier picks the empty pot.

Roya R. Rad

A carpenter stops at the house with no door.

Workers rush toward some hint of emptiness, which they then start to fill.

Their hope, though, is for emptiness, so don't think you must avoid it. It contains what you need!

Dear soul, if you were not friends with the vast nothing inside, why would you always be casting your net into it, and waiting so patiently?

This invisible ocean has given you such abundance, but still you call it "death", that which provides you sustenance and work.

God has allowed some magical reversal to occur, so that you see the scorpion pit

as an object of desire, and all the beautiful expanse around it, as dangerous and swarming with snakes.

This is how strange your fear of death and emptiness is, and how perverse the attachment to what you want.

Now that you've heard me on your misapprehensions, dear friend, listen to Attar's story on the same subject.

He strung the pearls of this about King Mahmud, how among the spoils of his Indian campaign there was a Hindu boy, whom he adopted as a son.

He educated and provided royally for the boy and later made him vice-regent, seated

on a gold throne beside himself.

One day he found the young man weeping.

"Why are you crying? You're the companion of an emperor! The entire nation is ranged out before you like stars that you can command!"

The young man replied, "I am remembering my mother and father, and how they scared me as a child with threats of you!

'Uh-oh, he's headed for King Mahmud's court!

Nothing could be more hellish!' Where are they now when they should see me sitting here?"

This incident is about your fear of changing.

You are the Hindu boy. Mahmud, which means

Praise to the End, is the spirit's poverty or emptiness.

The mother and father are your attachment to beliefs and blood ties and desires and comforting habits.

Don't listen to them!
They seem to protect but they imprison.
They are your worst enemies.
They make you afraid of living in emptiness.
Some day you'll weep tears of delight in that court, remembering your mistaken parents!
Know that your body nurtures the spirit, helps it grow, and gives it wrong advice.
The body becomes, eventually, like a vest of chain mail in peaceful years, too hot in ummer and too cold in winter.
But the body's desires, in another way, are like an unpredictable associate, whom you must be patient with. And that companion is helpful, because patience expands your capacity to love and feel peace.
The patience of a rose close to a thorn keeps it fragrant. It's patience that gives milk
to the male camel still nursing in its third year, and patience is what the prophets show to us.
The beauty of careful sewing on a shirt is the patience it contains.
Friendship and loyalty have patience as the strength of their connection.
Feeling lonely and ignoble indicates that you haven't been patient.
Be with those who mix with God as honey blends with milk, and say, "Anything that comes and goes, rises and sets, is not what I love." Else you'll be like a caravan fire left to flare itself out alone beside the road.

In the following poem, Rumi seems to be communicating the feeling one gets when she feels a true liberation. By getting rid of the dust of irrationality, ignorance, addictive behaviors, and being determined and true to oneself, one would be able to free herself into an expanded sense of being.

Make yourself free from self at one stroke!
Like a sword, be without trace of soft iron;
Like a steel mirror, scour off all rust with contrition.

In the following, Rumi seems to be asking for the ultimate liberation, which is being free from any kind of mind- and soul-limiting belief and belonging.

Oh Beloved, take me.
Liberate my soul.
Fill me with your love and release me from the two worlds.
If I set my heart on anything but you let fire burn me from inside.
Oh Beloved, take away what I want.
Take away what I do.
Take away what I need.

Quotes

A human being is part of the whole called by us universe, a part limited in time and space. We experience ourselves, our thoughts and feelings as something separate from the rest. A kind of optical delusion of consciousness. This delusion is a kind of prison for us, restricting us to our personal desires and to affection for a few persons nearest to us. Our task must be to free ourselves from the prison by widening our circle of compassion to embrace all living creatures and the whole of nature in its beauty. The true value of a human being is determined by the measure and the sense in which they have obtained liberation from the self. We shall require a substantially new manner of thinking if humanity is to survive.
Albert Einstein

It is the natural and inherent impulse of life to seek to live more, it is the nature of each to extend its boundaries and find fuller expression.
Wattles

One can choose to go back toward safety or forward toward growth. Growth must be chosen again and again; fear must be overcome again and again.
Abraham Maslow

The true value of a human being is determined primarily by the measure and the sense in which he has attained liberation from the self.
Albert Einstien

Man unites himself with the world in the process of creation.
Erich Fromm

Chapter 6

Toward Self Determination

Rumi's writings seem to be coming from of a self-determined person. Self-determination means having the freedom to be in charge of our own life, choosing where we live, who we spend our time with, what we do, what we like, what our goals are, what our passion is, and how to best and most productively live our life. An immense part of self-determination is educating our self about facts to make responsible decisions. Self-determination theory focuses on the difference between behaviors that are self-determined and behaviors that are partially controlled in some manner. Individuals get more pleasure and benefit from activities if they have a sense that they are doing them from intrinsic interest instead of extrinsic reward. Individuals, who feel like their lives are conquered by what others think, and how they may be judged, may experience a feeling of inferiority and mental blockage for what seems to be a confused sense of self.

Believing we can control a major part of our own destiny is empowering. Having a responsible and determined attitude, as well as the ability to choose one's goals and walk toward those goals will give individuals a sense of integrity, meaning, and hope. Self-determination is more related to being in charge of our own life, but not necessarily living completely self-sufficiently and independently. It means making one's own choices with a strong mind, not a constantly changing and impulsive mind, one that works through reason and not responding unwisely or irrationally to impulsivity.

The ability to be self-determined is a practice that starts in childhood and persists throughout one's life. It involves developing and learning skills like being self aware, being assertive, being creative, having a healthy and balanced sense of self worth, being a good problem-solver, having a sense of self-respect, having boundaries, and balancing emotions, among many more. One needs to learn to be able to set goals, examine her options, and prioritize what is the most important aspect of her life at each stage, to be able to go through the process of self-determination.

The conscious self was explained in the previous chapters. To relate it to the content of this chapter, if we acknowledge and understand the conscious part of our self, it will go to work for us in the process of self-determination. The conscious self is capable of making decisions that are based on one's daily life, and has the intellectual abilities of using logic, memory, imagination, and emotions to comprehend situations and gain knowledge about one's self and surrounding. This will help the individual become more aware of her daily life, helping her look at how her actions and words have consequences, and how they affect her life. This process will help the individual analyze her intentions and actions by looking at her motivation, goals, ways to achieve these, and the consequences of each on her life. The conscious self should be in charge of organizing these different parts of one's life, in order for her to walk through the process of self-determination. Through self-knowledge, the conscious self will be able to act effectively, using one's personal abilities and life circumstances.

In the following poem, Rumi seems to be communicating the importance of a person's mental and focal maturation to be able to make the right choices in picking the most suitable route throughout life, since he mentions that there are many routes. He seems to be communicating with the reader that many get confused about what is the right way to go, and they limit themselves by choosing something of lower value to the self. Furthermore, he seems to say that for the real feeling of ecstasy, one has to go through the stages of self-awareness in order to be able to pick the route that brings a sense of true bliss. A sense of bliss that is not rooted in imitation, but comes from knowledge of reality, based on what is real, not a misapprehension. Other than that, any sense of ecstasy will be of worthless and temporary. (4)

God has given us a dark wine so potent that, drinking it, we leave the two worlds.
God has put into the form of hashish a power to deliver the taster from self-consciousness.
God has made sleep so that it erases every thought.
God made Majnun love Layla so much that just her dog would cause confusion in him.
There are thousands of wines that can take over our minds.
Don't think all ecstasies are the same!
Jesus was lost in his love for God.
His donkey was drunk with barley.
Drink from the presence of saints, not from those other jars.
Every object, every being, is a jar full of delight.
Be a connoisseur, and taste with caution.
Any wine will get you high.
Judge like a king, and choose the purest, the ones unadulterated with fear, or some urgency about "what's needed."

Quotes

The person in peak experiences feels himself, more than other times, to be the responsible, active, creating center of his activities and of his perceptions. He feels more like a prime-mover, more self-determined (rather than caused, determined, helpless, dependent, passive, weak, bossed). He feels himself to be his own boss, fully responsible, fully volitional, with more "free-will" than at other times, master of his fate, an agent.
Abraham Maslow

If you are irritated by every rub, how will you be polished?
Rumi

Little by little, wean yourself. This is the gist of what I have to say. From an embryo whose nourishment comes in the blood, move to an infant drinking milk, to a child on solid food, to a searcher after wisdom, to a hunter of invisible game.
Rumi

Only those who attempt the absurd will achieve the impossible.
Albert Einstein

Be occupied, then, with what you really value, and let the thief take something else.
Rumi

Chapter 7

Toward Self-Assertion

Rumi's writings seem to be communicating the concept psychologists call assertiveness. A person who wants to experience her true self, a person who wants to get rid of all deception, and one who wants to be liberated, actualized, determined, and discover herself must learn to respect and express herself. For a person to learn to respect herself, she must learn her boundaries, clarify them, and communicate them. Assertiveness is a tool for doing that.

There are basically three types of behavioral patterns that people use to relate to each other: Aggressive, passive, and assertive.

Aggression is related to dominance, wanting to take advantage of others, and crossing other people's boundaries. Aggressiveness is when one expresses her rights at the expense, deprivation, or embarrassment of another. Aggression can become emotionally or physically vigorous, not allowing the other person's rights to surface.

Passivity is submission to, and being invaded and devalued by others. Passivity happens when a person submits to another's dominance behavior, putting her own wishes and desires aside to pay attention to fulfilling the wishes and desires of the dominant partner.

However, assertiveness is the balanced form of the above two. Assertiveness is the ability for self-expression in healthy ways, without violating the rights of others and crossing their boundaries. Assertiveness is a straight, open, and sincere communication, which helps the individual feel a sense of self-enhancement, self-expression, and self-confidence. It also helps one to receive and give more respect. Expressing one's thoughts and feelings in a way that clearly communicates the person's needs and intentions is a great way for a person to experience her true self. In order to be able to get assertive, we must value ourselves. Being assertive is different than being selfish. Acting in selfish ways means that one is violating the rights of others, which are destructive and aggressive acts instead of constructive and assertive ones.

In the following poem, Rumi seems to be describing healthy boundaries, self-respect, assertiveness, healthy relationships, selective association, being knowledgeable about what we want, and having the ability to arrange our environment in a way that complements and is in harmony with our intentions in life. This includes the ability to self-express and communicate our needs and wants in life.

My heart, sit only with those who know and understand you.
Sit only under a tree that is full of blossoms.
In the bazaar of herbs and potions don't wander aimlessly find the shop with a potion that is sweet.
If you don't have a measure people will rob you in no time.
You will take counterfeit coins thinking they are real.
Don't fill your bowl with food from every boiling pot you see.
Not every joke is humorous, so don't search for meaning where there isn't one.
Not every eye can see, not every sea is full of pearls.
My heart, sing the song of longing Like nightingale. The sound of your voice casts a spell
on every stone, on every thorn.
First, lay down your head then one by one let go of all distractions.
Embrace the light and let it guide you beyond the winds of desire.
There you will find a spring and nourished by its see waters like a tree, you will bear fruit forever.

Quotes

Jesus said, "If you bring forth what is within you, what you bring forth will save you. If you do not bring forth what is within you, what you do not bring forth will destroy you."
Thich Nhat Hanh

Nobody can hurt me without my permission.
Gandhi

Don't let your throat tighten with fear. Take sips of breath all day and night, before death closes your mouth.
Rumi

As human beings, our greatness lies not so much in being able to remake the world—that is the myth of the atomic age—as in being able to remake ourselves.
Gandhi

The true antidote to greed is contentment. If you have a strong sense of contentment, it doesn't matter whether you obtain the object of your desire or not. Either way, you are still content.
Gyatso

Chapter 8

Toward Self Discipline

Looking through how a healthy sense of self can be accomplished, and how one can experience all the pieces of herself as a whole, it becomes apparent that self-discipline is a needed tool. If we respond to every sense of desire, if we live a limitless life with no boundaries, if we shape our mind according to a valueless life, and if we are still stuck in the concept of instant gratification; then we may be leading a life of continuous struggle, pain, wasted power, hopelessness, and helplessness.

Self-discipline is the capability to be decisive and to take a productive action despite the emotional state one is in, at any given point of time. A self-disciplined person is training herself to be at a point where, when she makes a conscious decision, she will follow it. Self-discipline will help the person overcome any addictive behaviors, procrastination, disorganization, and ignorance.

Mental and emotional discipline is similar to muscle strengthening. The more one trains it, the stronger it will get. We also have to consider the fact that people possess different degrees of self-discipline, depending on who they are. The fundamental way to become more self-disciplined is to undertake challenges that one can successfully complete, but are also close to one's limits.

We discussed the terms child and conscious selves in previous chapters. To relate these to self-discipline, if we are trained and mastered by the conscious self, it helps us develop freely while disciplining ourselves. On the other hand, if we let the child self be in control, we will be a wild horse running away with no sense of direction.

When we function from our conscious self, we will have an inner sense of freedom while regulating ourselves. But discipline imposed by others may be resented. If we do not learn to adequately discipline ourselves, we will continue inflicting pain and harm on ourselves and others. Being free, we learn from our own experience how to control ourselves. If we do not learn this and get in the way of others, they may try to trigger a behavior in us as a way of self-defense.

The balance of living, points to the important factor that we have to learn to be in control of ourselves, and to be respectful of other people's autonomy and freedom. In order to do that, we need to learn ways to control our thoughts, emotions, perceptions, and behaviors. Self-discipline involves supervision of the child self by the conscious self, resulting in the child self's productivity through cooperating with the conscious self.

The child self seems to like rituals or routines that turn into habitual patterns of behavior, which are sometimes unconscious. The child self does not understand that when a behavior, thought, or emotion is damaging to us, we need to make changes. It just allow the damaging factor to repeat itself over and over again, without looking at the short and long term effects. It is searching for instant gratification. It prefers to stay in a comfort zone rather than learning and moving. This child and primitive self may obey and imitate what she perceives. If this child self is mistreated or ignored by the conscious self, or by others, it may go up against them in self defense. In order to change old non-functional habits, one must redirect and coach this child self through the conscious self. If the conscious self is not involved in disciplining, it may tolerate the child self by ignoring many habits that may not be valuable and productive, or may even be destructive. Every individual is responsible in providing a balance of affection and discipline to her child self through her conscious self.

Our life and awareness seem to have many dimensions beyond what is conscious in our minds. What psychologists call the subconscious and unconscious minds seem to be holding many subtle levels of awareness that have an effect on, and provide means for, our conscious self.

Disciplining the lower parts will result in them giving their control to the higher parts, which will lead to a more planned and reasonable life instead of an impulsive one. There have been many studies about self-discipline. They seem to be reporting that the ability to discipline one's self is an even stronger factor than intelligence when it comes to having a sense of balanced and successful life.

Regulating our behavior, thought, emotions, and mind, being in control of them rather than letting them have control over us, restraining them when they seem to be damaging us, and making them obey our core self are what self-discipline means. For example, people who are self-disciplined are, most of the time, able to know when to do what, and how much of it to do. Such people have a sense of inner power. They will usually not respond to instant gratification if doing so may have negative long-term consequences for them. They would plan their life to become more advanced and healthier, mentally, emotionally, and focally. Many times, if desires seem to have damaging long term consequences for them or what they value, they will control and regulate those desires and will act upon them in a rational, healthy and objective manner. Their life will have a sense of integrity to it because they will not make mistakes or errors intentionally, and because they stand up to their values.

Emotions, thoughts, and behaviors are like tools for us to develop, make progress, and evolve in the course of life. We have to have these tools in control, meaning that we have to be able to regulate them in a productive way that is functional for us. How each person goes about disciplining herself depends on her weaknesses, strengths, limitations, potentials, and goals, but practice takes one closer to one's regulated self. We cannot give in to our desires too much if they have negative consequences both short and long. For example, if we eat a chocolate every time we crave one, imagine what it will do to us. We may end up craving it more and more, to a point where it becomes uncontrollable. However, finding a balanced way to do it will satisfy our craving in a controlled fashion. At the end, it is all about controlling the desire, not vanishing it. There is no harm to a desire that is being managed.

The same is true with emotional desires. We cannot give in to every emotional desire we have. There has to be a balance, and there has to be a reassurance that fulfilling this desire will not have negative effects on us in the short and long runs. For example, too many time people, responding to their sexual desires impulsively, have caused themselves and their environment, damage beyond repair. Many diseases, many unwanted pregnancies, many children born to teenagers, child pornography, sexual abuse and assault, etc., are just some of the examples created by uncontrolled sexual desires.

Rumi, in the following poem, seems to be communicating with the reader the term "harsh for good," which could be related to how the process of self-discipline could be a difficult process, but a helpful and essential one. We need to train our mind, body, and self to have boundaries, live with rules and values, and follow the route of our passion, or else we will be lost in the limitless world.

I said, "Thou art harsh, like such a one."
"Know," he replied, "That I am harsh for good, not from rancor and spite."
"Whoever enters saying, 'This I,' I smite him on the brow;
"For this is the shrine of Love, O fool! It is not a sheep cote!
"Rub thine eyes, and behold the image of the heart."

Quotes

Knowing others is wisdom. Knowing the self is enlightenment. Mastering others is strength. Mastering the self is true power.
Lao-Tzu, Tao Te Ching

The greatest way to live with honor in this world is to be who we pretend to be.
Socrates

It is often tragic to see how blatantly a man bungles his own life and the lives of others, yet remains totally incapable of seeing how much the whole tragedy originates in himself, and how he continually feeds it and keeps it going.
Carl Jung

Brother, stand the pain. Escape the poison of your impulses. The sky will bow to your beauty, if you do. Learn to light the candle. Rise with the sun. Turn away from the cave of your sleeping. That way a thorn expands to a rose. A particular glows with the universal.
Rumi

Little by little, through patience and repeated effort, the mind will become stilled in the Self.
Bhagavad Gita

Two purposes in human nature rule. Self-love to urge, and reason to restrain.
Alexander Pope

I count him braver who overcomes his desires than him who conquers his enemies; for the hardest victory is over self.
Aristotle

Chapter 9

Toward Emotional Stability

In Rumi's writings, he seems to be expressing a number of feelings that he is experiencing intensely. He seems to be aware of his emotions and experiencing them as they are. There are combinations of feelings that he seems to be communicating from joy to sadness. When we experience something painful and threatening, we encounter emotional pain. These feelings may give us a sense of helplessness. People who live through these without acknowledging them are troubled by anxiety, nightmares, and troubling memories after the event itself is long past. This lack of skill to deal with the emotional pain affects a person's sense of feeling safe in this world, and may set in motion a series of questions concerning life, its meaningfulness, and its unfairness.

It's important for a person to take time to mirror her painful experiences and to acknowledge the reality of this pain. It is also useful to normalize this pain in the sense of understanding that many others experience these painful feelings too. After that awareness comes the beginning of the repairing process in total earnestness. One of the mistakes that people make about emotional pain is that they think that this pain is "not a big deal, and it will pass on by itself." They feel like there is something uniquely wrong with their feelings, or often they begin to compare themselves with others, disregarding how each individual may be unique to her own experience.

The human body is a phenomenal mechanism. This is true for both physiological and mental mechanisms, which seem to reflect one another. The human psyche, like the human body, has natural emotional healing procedures built in. For example, in many ways, crying makes the person feel better afterwards, but emotional wounds that are not attended to or healed cause a large amount of psychological pain for the person for years and years, and maybe even a lifetime.

Emotional pain is like physiological pain. For example, if you treat cancer cells at an early stage, the chances of healing are much greater than if you treat them later. Pain, both emotional and physiological, can be endured up to a point, but can be devastating if experienced excessively and for too long.

Psychologists recommend that it is useful to acknowledge our feelings, but this has to be done with caution. Healing our wounds should be done at a proper time and in a safe place, with people we trust.

Everyone is unique in the way they respond to the healing process.

Emotions are the core source of being vibrant, and, if blocked, can be a major source of stress, suffering, confusion, and pain. Encountering one's feelings within one's comfort level is the safest way to go about the healing process. A person who is emotionally healthy is able to feel emotions intensely, can identify and comprehend feelings, and the needs related to those feelings, has self-assertive and self-soothing skills, and is capable of forming intimate relationships in which boundaries are respected. Such a person has a sense of commitment to what she values, and allows herself to be human and normal, capable of making mistakes and learning from them.

The following poem by Rumi which is a Coleman Bark's translation seems to be communicating the concept of emotional stability, in a way. As one reads the poem, it seems like Rumi is encouraging the reader to welcome all her emotions as they occur, experiencing them, processing them, analyzing them, and recognizing that these emotions exist for a reason. After that, a way of finding an inner balance of emotions will be easier.

> *This being human is a guest house.*
> *Every morning a new arrival.*
> *A joy, a depression, a meanness, some momentary awareness comes*
> *As an unexpected visitor.*
> *Welcome and entertain them all!*
> *Even if they're a crowd of sorrows, who violently sweep your house empty of its furniture, still treat each guest honorably.*
> *He may be clearing you out for some new delight.*
> *The dark thought, the shame, the malice, meet them at the door laughing, and invite them in.*
> *Be grateful for whoever comes, because each has been sent as a guide from beyond.*

Quotes

Truth is by nature self-evident. As soon as you remove the cobwebs of ignorance that surround it, it shines clear.
Gandhi

No matter how busy you may think you are, you must find time for reading, or surrender yourself to self-chosen ignorance.
Confucius

I count him braver who overcomes his desires than him who conquers his enemies; for the hardest victory is over self.
Aristotle

Be the change you want to see in the world.
Gandhi

Nobody can hurt me without my permission.
Gandhi

Chapter 10

Healing & Self Knowledge

Rumi seems to have been able to find his own therapy, healing, and analysis tools, which are reflected in his poems and writings. He seems to have been aware of his emotional and focal being and seems to have been able to express himself through his writings.

However, everyone can be aware of herself. Many people are not aware of emotional pain in themselves, or that of others. For example, they may ask, "Why can't she just get out of this depression?"

Sometimes it is easier to stay in that jammed state than to come out and face reality. It is this fear of reality that makes us escape from our pain, hide from it, deny it, and project it, rather than try to find a cure for it. Sometimes, we would do anything to keep the focus away from ourselves. We focus the camera on everything and everyone except ourselves. It seems like the emotional pain becomes a part of our comfort zone, not because we like it, but because we are getting used to it and because we do not have the courage or the determination to step out of it.

Change of any kind appears scary, difficult, and perhaps even impossible. The irrational patterns of feelings, thinking, perceptions, and behaviors that a person with emotional pain experiences and expresses are not at a conscious level most of the time. They are usually out of awareness. Root-oriented treatment starts at this subconscious level to help the person become aware of what is happening. It helps the person become insightful about herself.

As mentioned in previous chapters, the less aware humans are of their motives, intentions, feelings, thoughts, actions, and perceptions; the more these components control them, rather than them having control over these parts of their being. As an example, consider the aggressive person who has allowed her emotion of anger to control her life rather than having control over this emotion. This person is moving through life being run over by her anger, without realizing that this same emotion was supposed to be used in a balanced form called assertiveness for survival and progress in life. This lack of control gets her stuck in repeating the same destructive patterns over and over again, without seeing the effect they have on her, and the directions of life they are taking her towards. For such a person, relief from this sense of being unaware can start with realizing and integrating that which is being masked into her everyday consciousness. That is when the process of "cleaning the mirror of being," a phrase Rumi uses throughout his poems, commences.

The process of mirror-cleaning is a very personal and unique one, depending on the person's individuality and frame of mind. We have to start taking the dust off the mirror of our being. Then, and only then, will it reflect us as we really are—an image of our true self. We also have to start the process of becoming conscious of our particular personality process. We have to be able to realize that parts of us may need or want things that make the rest of us feel let down. And, above all, we have to picture for ourselves how all these pieces of our self fit together, like a puzzle. Books, lectures, websites, and other forms of self-help tools are general and valuable for a person looking for self-education, but they are like statistics. They will give us a general idea about most people, but we have to remember that each of us is a unique individual, and treatment for our healing process and growth will have to be administered accordingly. We have to keep in mind that it is never too late to start the process, and that determination and hope are the keys to this door. In this poem, Rumi seems to be communicating a sense of acceptance he felt toward what is yet to come, because he had come to know himself. He seems to be expressing his belief of how humans are constantly in the process of change and development. (2)

> *I died from minerality and became vegetable;*
> *And from vegetativeness I died and became animal.*
> *I died from animality and became man.*
> *Then why fear disappearance through death?*
> *Next time I shall die*
> *Bringing forth wings and feathers like angels;*
> *After that, soaring higher than angels,*
> *What you cannot imagine,*
> *I shall be that.*

Quotes

Please, do not visualize that we exist above you, such as in heaven. The concepts above and below are products of your mind. The soul does not swing upwards. It exists in the center and orients itself in every direction.
Hans Bender

The core of my personality consists of many selves.
Hans Bender

Meanings are not determined by situations, but we determine ourselves by the meanings we give to situations.
Alfred Adlre

If you want to truly understand something, try to change it.
Kurt Lewin

There is no certainty; there is only adventure.
Roberto Assagioli

Chapter 11

Pyramid of Growth

The pyramid of self-discovery and growth starts at the most basic level and goes up to higher levels. Some researchers estimate that only about two percent of population will go all the way to the top of the pyramid and become self-actualized, and even fewer can go to its highest level of self-transcend. However, this does not mean that people cannot reach these levels. It just means that they have to put their focus on it.

During the course of our lifetime, we continuously ask ourselves what is the meaning of our life? Which direction are we taking, and where we are heading? Let us climb the mountain of self-actualization and self-growth. Again, as Jung might say, "The purpose of life is to recognize the self." After accomplishing this most important task, the rest of life will come together like the pieces of a puzzle. Climbing a mountain takes focus, determination, effort, skill, and hope. We cannot settle for anything less than our full potential, and we do not know what our full potential is until we learn who we truly are. We are multifaceted human beings and need to celebrate and discover this.

Going through the process of self-growth will lead us to turn into individuals who give more than they take from this life, while at the same time feeling at peace with themselves. That is when we become one with the whole picture of creation, and that is when we see ourselves as a drop in the ocean of being, affecting it and being affected by it every single moment of every single day. That is called true awareness; being aware of our actions, our thoughts, and our emotions at all times.

In order to more clearly understand humans, these complex designs which are each unique in their own way, I formed a Systematic Transformational Psychology (STP) based on natural observation of clients as well as intense literature review. This concept is based on a number of theories including that of Abraham Maslow, Carl Jung, Existential Psychology, and Client Centered Psychology, to name a few. It is a multimodal approach to understanding human's nature. STP explains that humans need to grow physically, emotionally, mentally, intellectually, and spiritually in order to go through the process of life in a healthy and natural way while being fruitful, productive, and fertile. Knowing about this process, and learning about each stage of life and what it means can help humans to be able to move forward in self growth and to reach their full potential by giving them the tool of awareness. What this full potential is, is different for each individual and this is where Carl Jung and Existential concepts come into play to help individuals learn about themselves to learn their strengths, weaknesses, limitations, and talents by discovering themselves and all their elements including their conscious and unconscious ones. This learning leads to awareness. Being aware while moving forward in life will help individuals lessen wasting useful power, refocus on what is really important at each stage, prioritize, increase productivity, and release unleashed potentials while having a focus in life at all times.

To understand the process more lets explain Abraham **Maslow's** hierarchy, first. He wrote an article titled <u>A Theory of Human Motivation</u> which appeared in Psychological Review, in 1943. This article then turned into his book titled <u>Toward a Psychology of Being</u>. In his writings, Abraham Maslow formulated a need-based framework of human motivation based on his clinical experience with clients. Today, this theory is popular with modern leaders and executive managers to find means of employee motivation for workforce management but it can also be useful in understanding anyone's motivations and intentions behind a behavior.

Maslow states that humans are motivated by unsatisfied needs and that certain lower needs need to be satisfied before higher needs can be attended. He said that the general needs of physiological, safety, love, and esteem have to meet and fulfilled before a person is able to act unselfishly. He categorized these needs as deficiency needs. When a person is able to fulfill these basic needs, s/he continues to move up the ladder of growth toward self actualization. The satisfaction of these needs are healthy while preventing their gratification without replacing them with something healthy may create illness or evil acts in a person consciously or unconsciously.

As a result, for adequate self discovery process, it is important that individuals understand which needs are active for them and what creates their motivation in life in order to understand their intentions behind their behavior. This will help them get more in tuned with their unconscious mind. Maslow's model indicates that in general basic, low-level needs such as physiological requirements and safety must be satisfied before higher-level needs such as self-fulfillment are pursued. As depicted in this hierarchical diagram, sometimes called 'Maslow's Needs Pyramid' or 'Maslow's Needs Triangle', when a need is satisfied, it no longer motivates and the next higher need takes its place. Here is a brief description:

Level 1: Biological and Physiological needs. Basic life needs like air, food, drink, shelter, warmth, sex, homeostasis, breathing, water, excretions, etc.

Level 2: Safety needs. Protection, security, order, law, limits, stability, personal security, financial security, health and well being, safety net against accidents/illness and adverse impacts.

Level 3: Belonging and love needs. Family, affection, relationships, work group, social/cultural/religious groups, friendship, intimacy, having a supportive and communicative groups to belong to, giving and receiving love.

Level 4: Esteems needs met by external factors. Achievement, status, responsibility, reputation, recognition, attention, social status.

Level 5: Esteems needs met by internal factors, accomplishment, self respect, inner sense of contentment with one's self.

Level 6: Self Actualization. Personal growth and fulfillment, truth, justice, wisdom, meaning in life, peak experiences, energized, harmony, always finding opportunities to grow, striving for full potential, awareness of self. According to Maslow, only 2% get to be here not because they can not but because they get stuck at fulfilling the lower needs.

Level 6 (deeper into it): Need for Aesthetics and knowledge. Maslow later added this as a part of self actualization but further down that level. .

Level 7: Self Transformation. This is where the individual experiences the ultimate state of inner liberation being free from the concept of "self" and living from being connected to something bigger. This is where the individual gets free from anxious attachments, neediness, irrational thinking, unbalanced emotions, impulses, and being dragged by the ego. Perhaps, something like what some of the prophets reported to have experienced.

It is important to note that Maslow's pyramid and the experiences related to each level are different for different individuals. Some individuals may be capable of moving faster, slower, not at all, or jumping from one to the other depending on their unique personalities, abilities, limitations, strengths, and innately born talents. In addition, some individuals have the ability to replace an unmet need with something positive to fulfill its empty feeling. It all goes back to the concept of self awareness, self discovery, and finding that unique way that works for each individual. What this pyramid helps with is the self awareness process, once we understand our unconscious motives; we are more easily able to make changes.

What remains the same for everyone is the fact that we all have needs and have to find healthy ways to acknowledge and process these needs and move on. An unmet and unacknowledged need can cause obstacles in growth. In some instances, we see individuals whose unacknowledged needs have made them hypocrites. In spite of this, needs should not be mistaken for the concepts of desire and instant gratification. Instant gratification is an impulsive reaction to a desire, without considering the short and long term consequences. As mentioned before, desire by itself is not something we can label as bad or good; it is when we don't have control over it, cannot stop the urges, and can not delay an instant gratification that make desires wounding. It all goes back to the same concept, the ability for inner control. However, if we respond to desires responsibly, there is no harm. But desire is not the same thing as need, they are two different concepts.

We have used the term instant gratification a few times, an instant gratification is an inborn trait that has been with us since childhood. When we are born, we do not have the ability to hold an urge. We get hungry, we cannot delay it, and we want food right then and there. We get thirsty, we want water. We cry to communicate that we need these, and will not stop until the desire if fulfilled. However, as we grow older and have more control over our environment, we learn, or should learn, to delay a desire and evaluate whether it is good or bad for us.

Unfortunately, if we are not able to delay gratification and respond to a desire instantly, we may pay a high price for fulfilling it. But does the cost outweigh the benefit? This is the question that one needs to ask before responding to an urge. The more mature one becomes, the more capable she becomes in analyzing the deeper consequences of her actions.

In the process of self-growth, we have to be aware of each state we are in. This will prevent us from being trapped in one area of our life.

Life, after all, is a process that needs continuous progress and change. It's like a river that needs to flow to stay fresh and full of life. This process seems like going through school and seeking a higher degree. The higher the degree, the more difficult it gets, but at the same time the person has more skills, intelligence, and strength to deal with the difficulties.

By graduating from each level and going to the next, it seems like one's mind and core being are expanding. We can relate the process of self-growth to climbing a mountain. Reaching the top of the mountain needs strength, motivation, and determination. It also needs strong muscles that are built during practice and training. With each step up, muscles contract and expand, getting ready for the next one. As one climbs higher up the mountain, she sees everything below with a more expanded vision. The same applies to a person's psych. As one goes up the pyramid of self-growth, one gets internally stronger, more evolved, and ready for the next level, while becoming more capable of accepting challenges and what is about to come.

The first few levels are self-explanatory, starting with needs for survival and a healthy sense of physical self. The middle levels are the need for self-esteem, which start with the need for admiration, respect, and love from others. Once one grows out of this and becomes confident enough, all one needs is feeling good about herself without reliance on the outside world. At this level, one's definition of herself and how she feels is not defined by the outside world but by how she feels inside.

After that comes the self-actualization level. At this level, one has the instinctive need to make the most of her capacity, and to make every effort to be the best she can. It is the intrinsic growth of what is already in every organism, including humans. Other organisms do this based on instinct, but humans are the most evolved organisms, and have free will. This free will can work in opposite ways. It can take them to the top, or it can keep them at the bottom of the pyramid. In either case, it will be a choice.

After the self esteem levels comes self-actualization. We discussed self-actualization previously, but, to elaborate, some characteristics of self-actualized people are that they embrace facts and realities of the world rather than denying or avoiding them, are spontaneous, are creative, are good problem-solvers who use reason, focus on the solution not the problem, appreciate life in general with all its ups and downs, have a system of morality that is fully internalized and independent of external authority, and are aware, open, honest, free, and trustworthy.

Finally, the last level of the pyramid is self-transcendence. Some identify this as the ultimate spirituality. It is worth noting that only a very small percentage of people will get to this level. Again, this is not because they are not capable, but rather it is because these people get trapped in fulfilling the lower level needs of the pyramid and suppress, avoid, or deny their higher needs. At this self-transcendence level, many people have peak experiences which are unifying and ego–transcending, which brings a sense of purpose and integration to the individual. This level may be what many prophets and people who affected life greatly, in a positive way, and have continued to have a positive effect even after their death, have reached. Based on Rumi's writings and biography, it seems like he might have been able to reach this level as well. Rumi writes:

Our beyond ideas of wondering and right doing, there is a field. I will meet you there.

When one walk though the pyramid of growth, one reaches a place when she, by design, forms a format of giving back to her surroundings. This act of giving back comes more naturally as one becomes a more true form of herself. Acts of giving and learning how to become productive members of society are important parts of the process of self-growth. Looking at psychological aspects of the old saying that it is better to give than to receive indicates that acts of giving usually enhance the bond between the giver and the receiver. It tells us about ourselves, and gives us a sense of competence which makes us feel good. According to Erich Fromm, a well known psychologist, most humans want to be loved, but it is actually the act of loving that is gratifying. We want to be loved because it helps our chances to love and to be connected with others.

Every time we give something or do something for others, we feel useful, generous, and kind. These are all positive feelings that help nurture us. Charitable giving is not usually a separate act from the individual's sense of self. It seems to be a part of a group of personality traits, including selflessness, high-mindedness, and kindness. The development of generosity can often be rooted in the childhood experiences. Starting in childhood, one needs to be provided an environment in which one is given opportunities to give to others to build a sense of compassion. The act of giving helps children experience the joy of sharing and serving something larger than themselves. The biggest barrier to generosity is our own selfish temperament and, to some degree, our wounded self. Unless we deal with this fundamental dilemma and learn to overcome it, we can never move up too far on the Ladder of Generosity.

Rambam, a 12th century Jewish scholar, wrote about the act of giving in her writing. She writes what is titled the Rambam's Ladder, which provides grounds for why we can become more enhanced people by giving in healthier ways. In her writings, she developed an eight-step program on giving to the poor on the basis of Jewish law. She explained that the lowest level of the ladder represents giving begrudgingly, for example giving money to a panhandler. The highest step represents the ability of self reliance, for example offering the panhandler a job, so he doesn't need to beg anymore, or even further educating the panhandler about the importance of having a job. Therefore, it seems like even the act of giving has levels that will be opened to a person who is working through the process of self growth. (13)

In the following poem, Rumi seems to be communicating the importance of connecting with others. He writes:*

How very close
How very close
is your soul with mine
I know for sure
everything you think
goes through my mind

I am with you
now and doomsday
not like a host
caring for you at a feast alone
with you I am happy
all the times
the time I offer my life
or the time
you gift me your love
offering my life
is a profitable venture
each life I give
you pay in turn
a hundred lives again
in this house
there are a thousand
dead and still souls
making you stay
as this will be yours
a handful of earth
cries aloud
I used to be hair, or
I used to be bones
and just the moment
when you are all confused
leaps forth a voice
hold me close
I'm love and
I'm always yours

Quotes

It is often tragic to see how blatantly a man bungles his own life and the lives of others, yet remains totally incapable of seeing how much the whole tragedy originates in himself, and how he continually feeds it and keeps it going.
Carl Jung

Self-observation is essential to self-growth. You must first understand the motives for your own actions in order to understand others.
Chin Ning Chu

The greatest mistake a man can ever make is to be afraid of making one.
Elbert Hubbard

Self-observation is essential to self-growth. You must first understand the motives of your own actions in order to understand others.
Chin Ning Chu

Remember, the entrance door to the sanctuary is inside you.
Rumi

What was said to the rose that made it open was said to me here in my chest.
Rumi

It is every man's obligation to put back into the world at least the equivalent of what he takes out of it.
Albert Einstein

Think of giving not as a duty but as a privilege.
John D. Rockefeller Jr.

I have found that among its other benefits, giving liberates the soul of the giver.
Maya Angelou

In this world of trickery, emptiness is what your heart wants.
Rumi

In silence there is eloquence. Stop weaving and watch how the pattern improves.
Rumi

Conclusion

This book's attempt was to find a bridge between the language of spirituality and that of psychology. I am not sure where the two were separated but they really are not. When we go back to the meaning of the word, psychology is the study of psych. The word psych means spirit which would make psychology the study of spirit.

In modern days, it seems like more and more people are looking into a deep oriented psychology for answers toward their spiritual needs. As individuals evolve, their thirst for understanding expands and they look into ways of learning that make sense. More and more people are stepping out of imitation and want to find their own individual and unique path of life.

This book used Carl Jung when discussing the psychology of self. Carl Jung's school of thought is labeled as analytical psychology which in its depth is communicating the psychology of self. Carl Jung, who was a psychiatrist and a Freud follower at the beginning, ended up criticizing some of Freud's concepts and developing or modifying them. He, however, remained respectful of Freud. Carl Jung has been able to explain the deepest concepts of psychology known to humans, as of today. He explains humans as multifaceted. He reports that in order for one to learn about each facet, one has to dig in and discover all the opposite aspects of herself including the repressed memories of the shadow. Jung is able to explain many unanswered questions of psychology in a language that more and more people, interested in self discovery, find themselves relating to. Whereas before only people categorizing themselves as intellectuals seemed to have a thirst for his knowledge. The concepts that Carl Jung discusses are the ones that he has learned through years of natural observation, studies, literature reviews, and personal knowledge. Interestingly enough, some of his concepts can be observed in Rumi's poems. Carl Jung has written a number of bestselling books and hundreds of articles.

This book also uses Rumi's poems to give a new taste to the concept of self and its discovery process. When it comes to Rumi, he was barely known in the West until about 15 years ago but is now reported to be one of the most read poets in America. It seems like Rumi is able to put in words the highly personal and sometimes puzzling spiritual growth in a direct and comprehendible form. He seems to be able to talk to everyone without offending them. Rumi's poems seem to communicate with us a sense of faithfulness, perhaps enlightenment, encouraging the liberation of the higher self from the slavery to the false self or the ego. A false self that has unlimited desires of and attachments to the material world and can never stop unless mastered.

Both Rumi and Carl Jung, each one in their own language of poem and science, seem to be communicating that a true spiritual practice would be striving at transforming the compulsiveness of this false self and surrendering to a higher level of being. Without this, the person will be dragged by the ego and will live a life full of conflict because of the inconsistencies and ambiguity of impulses of the ego. In that case, the ego cannot benefit from the guidance and the nourishment of the higher self. It is further noted from these readings that the human that is not aware of her state of being and not moving forward toward maturation lives in a state of slavery to the false self and the unlimited desires of the materials world. While there is nothing wrong with gaining a moderate level of pleasure from this material world but the whole point is being in control and able to be its master rather than letting it run us.

A spiritual practice aims at transforming the compulsiveness of the false self and giving in to a higher order of reality. Without this giving in, the real self will be nothing more than a slave to the ego and lives in a state of internal conflict because of the contradictory impulses of the ego. The ego is cut off from the rest of the person's being and cannot benefit from the guidance and nourishment which can be provided from this source. One needs the power and determination to overcome this imprisonment to be able to realize her true humanity. When one is able to realize that she is something more than just the ego, perhaps something even divine and blissful that is a nurturing friend, what maybe called a transpersonal identity which is a part of all of us that lives with us and within us, may come out to awareness.

Relating these two extra ordinary human beings one from the East and the other from the West, one using a poetic language while the other using psychological language, about seemingly they same matter; has been an exciting journey for me as an author, one full of creativity and learning. I hope you enjoyed reading it as much as I enjoyed writing it.

Reference

1) Ibrahim Gamard. Retrieved on Jan/2007 from http://www.dar-almasnavi.org/about-the-translator.html

2) Translation by Jonathan Star

3) Memories, Dreams, and Reflections. The Autobiography of Dr. Carl Jung

4) Rumi, in *The Essential Rumi*, translated by Coleman Barks

5) The Portable Jung. An essay collection edited by Joseph Campbell

6) Translation by Andrew Harvey

7) American Psychiatric Association: *Diagnostic and Statistical Manual of Mental Disorders*, Fourth Edition. Washington, DC: American Psychiatric Association, 1994. See Appendix B: Criteria Sets and Axes Provided for Further Study, *Defensive Functioning Scale* (pp. 751–757).

8) Joly Lee (1973). The Colors of Love.

9) http://www.khamush.com/passion.htm

10) Translation by R. A. Nicholson

11) Rumi.org, *Persian Poems*. An anthology of verse translations, edited by A. J. Arberry, Everyman's Library, 1972 R. A. Nicholson

12) Rumi.org, Rumi VI (1369-1420) from Rumi: *One-Handed Basket Weaving*

13) Rumi.org, Mathnawi IV, 2683-96, *The Essential Rumi*, Coleman Barks.

14) Rambam's Ladder: A Meditation on Generosity and Why It Is Necessary to Give. By Julie Salamon.

Poems from the books, *Essential Rumi and Soul of Rumi,* both translated by Coleman Barks, and *Thief of Sleep* translated by Shahram Shiva.

Figure 1. From www.econsultant.com/articles/abraham-maslow-h...

*Any paragraph with a star at the end indicates that the writer had the information in her possession, but was unable to find the source. If you have the source, please write to us at info@SKBFPublishing.com

SKBF Publishing

(Self Knowledge Base/Foundation Publishing)
www.SKBFPublishing.com

SKBF Publishing is a publishing company dedicated to providing educational information for enhancing lifestyles and helping to create a more productive world through more aware individuals. Our task is to help awareness overcome ignorance. Our publishing focus is on research-oriented books, including subjects related to education, parenting, self improvement, psychology, spirituality, science, culture, finance, mental and physical health, and personal growth. We try to analyze each book carefully, and to choose the books we feel have reliable and valid information based on available research or the credential of the author.

Our mission is to publish information that expands understanding and promotes learning, compassion, self-growth, and a healthy sense of self, which leads to a healthier lifestyle. Our vision is to make a difference in people's lives by providing informative material that is reliable or research-oriented. SKBF Publishing is honored to have the helping hand of a number of scientist, educators, researchers, intellectuals, and scholars working together to review the books before approval for publishing with SKBF.

About the Author

Dr. Rohani Rad has a Doctorate in Clinical Psychology and a Masters in Applied Psychology. She is a member of American Psychological Association (APA), Virginia Psychological Association, and Applied Psychological Association.

In addition, she is the founder of a not-for-profit foundation (www.SelfKnowledgeBase.com) with the sole task of bringing awareness to a wide variety of subjects ranging from root-oriented understanding of global peace to child abuse. This foundation aims to be a bridge of understanding between the East and the West by generating research-oriented material and awareness.

Dr. Rad is also a researcher, and is actively involved with a number of studies related to emotional wellbeing, children's mental health, and relationships, among others. These studies are performed in both the Eastern and the Western sides of the globe for a broader perspective of factual information.

Dr. Rad has written a number of recognized and up-to-the-point books about the subjects of self-discovery, self-growth, and self-awareness from a psychological perspective. You can find more information about the author and her books on her website at www.OnlineHealthClinic.com

Food for Thought

Basic survival needs of humans include water, food, shelter, basic hygiene, health care.

Basic dignified needs of humans include education, work, freedom, security, justice, access to gaining their free will.

Life is inner connected, we are all affected by each other, in the short or long run. No step to make a root oriented change is a small step. Drops of water add up to form an ocean.

A poem by the author, Roya R. Rad

Inner Freedom

Freedom is a special inner concession
We can have access by self-confession

When the door of wakefulness unlocks
When we get rid of any sort of blocks

Something pours, some form of a drift
As if we let go of a long time heavy lift

We feel lighter and lighter
The outlook looks brighter

Our vision becomes more clear
As we learn to release our fear

Fear of rejection, fear of isolation
Turn into a complete sense of admiration

We get to a center place in creation
Where there is no sense of frustration

It is were we belong, there is no temptation
All that is, is a feeling of dedication

It is where we glance from the above
That we know what it means to feel love

The love was with us all along
We were just distracted for too long

Other books by this author

Book 1:
There is one religion:
The religion of KNOW THYSELF.

This book attempts to answer those seemingly ordinary questions of life with deep factual/practical answers. How do I get to my core being? Who am I? What do I do with my religion, culture, environment, family, gender, childhood etc., and how should I interact with these aspects of my identity? I feel like I have no use for some of these concepts. Do I need to learn about them, and if so, why? How do I put meaning to my life? What do I do with my emotional baggage? Others say I have it all, so why do I feel empty, sometimes? Why do I have such an emotional pain and can't cure it? I have so many people around me, so why do I feel lonely sometimes?

In this book there is a case example of an individual who learned about her culture, religion, and family background to ease her self-growth process. An individual who moved from East to West in her teen life, and used her immigration experience as a blessing, considering herself privileged to have had experienced living in two seemingly different countries in her lifetime..She came to learn that this experience had expanded her mind and thought in ways that would not have been possible if she had not immigrated. She also learned ways to learn and acknowledge the aspects of her life that she had escaped from, and found the experience fulfilling and uplifting. She felt a sense of having control over her life, picking what works, getting rid of whatever conditioning does not serve her, and choosing her own destiny.

Whatever we hold, we have to learn about and experience. Only after that we can make an informed decision about letting go of what does not work. If we let go of anything before learning and processing, we are getting ourselves into avoidance and repression rather than freedom. We can't ignore the rules and expect good results.

Book 2:
A Therapy Dialogue

A session-by-session therapy dialogue with an educated client who went through the self-actualization and self-growth processes. This book walks the reader through the process of therapy. In a step-by-step guide, it discusses what it means to live a life of "false self" and how to find a sense of "real self". It discusses a wide variety of issues like anxiety, family relationships, romantic relationships, negative behaviors and emotions and how to get rid of them, how to get to our full potential, what happiness really means, what is the difference between love and anxious attachment, what is assertiveness, how to process suppressed memories, and how to be able to see deeper into people's intentions, not just their behavior.

Book 3:
A concise comparison of theorists including Carl Jung and Abraham Maslow's concepts of the psyche and the self.

Finding a common ground between Carl Jung's general concepts of individuation, wholeness, spirituality and religion and those of Maslow's including his self Actualization and homeostasis concepts. (Out in 2010)

Book 4:
Where is my place in this world?

From egotistical to altruistic way of existence.

This book explains how to move above and beyond one's conditioning to get access to an unrepressed and infinite state of being where one can see that everything is inner connected and there is no separation. To get there one must increase her level of understanding and put her life to practice. The more one experiences life with awareness and knowledge, the closer she gets to her wholeness and that unlimited potential she beholds.

SKBF Publishing
Self Knowledge Base/Foundation Publishing

www.SKBFPublishing.com
Expanding your mind, widening your world, awakening your consciousness, and enhancing your life; one book at a time.

SKBF Publishing is a publishing company dedicated to providing educational information for enhancing lifestyles and helping to create a more productive world through more aware individuals. Our task is to help awareness overcome ignorance. Our publishing focus is on research-oriented and/or reliability contented books, including subjects related to education, parenting, self-improvement, psychology, spirituality, science, culture, finance, mental and physical health, and personal growth. We try to analyze each book carefully and to choose the books we feel have reliable and valid information based on available research or the credentials of the author. Our team of experts review every manuscript submitted to us for its practicality and content.

Our mission is to publish information that expands understanding and promotes learning, compassion, self-growth, and a healthy sense of self which leads to a healthier lifestyle. Our vision is to make a difference in people's lives by providing informative material that is reliable or research-oriented. SKBF Publishing is honored to have the helping hand of a number of scientist, educators, researchers, intellectuals, and scholars working together to review the books before approval for publishing with S